Jami
Don't look...

OUR LITTLE SECRET

KIERSTEN MODGLIN

xo.

KIERSTEN
MODGLIN
Love, Loss, & Lies

www.kierstenmodglinauthor.com
Cover Design: Tadpole Designs
Editing: Three Owls Editing
Proofreading: My Brother's Editor
Formatting: Tadpole Designs
First Print Edition: 2021
First Electronic Edition: 2021

For Emerald—
my best friend, closest confidant, the Michael to my Dwight, the
Maya to my Amy, and the one who somehow managed to dedicate
a book to me first.
(First of all, how dare you?!)
Same moon, friend.
This one's for you.

CHAPTER ONE

MICHELLE

I don't know what caused me to wake that night. Maybe it was the storm that had produced a noise outside—a limb breaking in the wind or the crash of thunder. Perhaps I knew something was amiss.

Either way, as soon as my eyes opened, my body sensed the shift. Somehow, I knew that something catastrophic was about to happen. That our lives as we knew them were about to change. I felt it in my very core, no matter how impossible that sounds.

Adrenaline coursed through my body, as if I'd just awoken from a nightmare or the sound of someone in the house, but that wasn't it. I sat up in bed, shaking and drenched in sweat as I reached out to wake Jude. I grabbed hold of his shoulder, rocking him back and forth until he stirred.

"Jude, wake up," I begged in a hurried whisper.

He rubbed his eyes, rolling over to look at me with just one eye open. Then he looked at the clock on the nightstand and back at me with a start.

"What is it? What's wrong?" he asked, his voice gruff with sleep.

"I don't know," I said honestly, my stomach tight with worry. I felt as if I were going to be sick. Tossing the covers back from my legs, I shivered as a chill ran over me, the cold air meeting the sweat on my skin. I moved to stand, scurrying across the room with intense trepidation.

Something is wrong.

Something is very, very wrong.

"What do you mean *you don't know?* It's nearly three in the morning. Where are you going?"

I pulled back the curtains, staring through the pane that had been spattered with raindrops from the ongoing storm. I squinted, glancing around our subdivision at the houses so similar to ours.

Southwest Acres was a small, elite subdivision just near the lake that ran through our town of Cason Glen. The six houses were nearly identical in layout and design, but different colors—varying shades of greens, browns, yellows, and blues throughout. We were surrounded entirely by woods, giving each home a private backyard. It had been designed as though the wilderness had come straight to our gates and stopped, leaving way for our tiny civilization.

We were only one of two subdivisions on this side of our lake, so we were guaranteed tranquility, safety, and, maybe most importantly, privacy.

Near the entrance of our cul-de-sac, I stared at the warm, amber light coming through the top window in the far corner of our mayor's home. At such a late hour, every window in Southwest Acres should've been dark. What was he doing up? Did he sense, like I had, that something was terribly wrong?

"Enzo's awake," I told Jude, who was sitting up in bed staring at his phone while still lazily rubbing his eye with his palm. "Looks like no one can sleep tonight." I ran my hand over my arm, trying to smooth the goose bumps. "I don't know what's going on, I can just feel it. Something's wrong. I need to go check on Caroline."

"Actually, you're right. Something is wrong. Something happened down by the lake," he said, standing from the bed with his phone pressed to his ear. "My phone must've woken you up. I don't know how I slept through it."

"What happened at the lake?"

He was silent for a moment, listening, then lowered his phone. "A wreck, maybe. Rodriguez is muffled in the voice-mail. It's…it's hard to hear over the storm. Either way, I have to get down there and figure out what's happening."

"A wreck? Oh my god. Is anyone hurt? Could you hear that much?" I asked, shivering slightly.

He wasn't listening as he zipped around the room, pulling on his uniform after he'd dropped his phone on the dresser.

"Jude? Did they say anyone was hurt?"

He buttoned his shirt and adjusted his badge, grabbing his tactical belt from the closet. "It doesn't sound like they know yet. I couldn't tell. I think he said someone crashed into the lake."

"Oh my god. What will you do? The storm is too bad to search. It's so dark…"

"I don't know. If they've just crashed on the bank but off the road, that's one thing, but if the car went into the lake…" He trailed off, stopping that train of thought. "We'll have to see what the damage is before I start thinking ahead. The storm may have caused someone to lose control. Let's just say a prayer it's nothing terrible." He zipped into the bath-room, swishing mouthwash quickly before turning to face me where I stood in the doorway, trying to make sense of it all. He kissed my lips, rushing past me while calling over his shoulder, "I've gotta go. I'll call when I can."

With that, he was down the stairs and out the door, and I was left alone. I wrapped a robe around my still-drenched clothing and walked down the hall, opening Caroline's door slowly, just to peek in on her. To my relief, she was there. Safe and sound. She'd curled up into a ball in the center of her bed, the way she'd slept since she was an infant, both hands tucked under her face.

I smiled, feeling comfort at seeing that she was secure in her room, that no harm had come to her, and that my bad feeling must've had everything to do with a nightmare I couldn't remember, Jude's phone ringing, and nothing else. With that, I closed the door again.

Then I made my way down the stairs and started a pot of coffee to help me wake up. There was no point in trying to sleep. I knew I wouldn't be able to until Jude made it back home. It was rare that I could sleep with him gone at all anymore, even when he'd taken the midnight shift. But the nights where he was called away were the worst.

As the sheriff of our small county of just under five thousand people, it wasn't as if he was constantly being called away in the middle of the night or that he was typically in danger during a shift, but that didn't make me worry any less when he was gone.

Once, I'd believed Cason County and, more importantly, our town of Cason Glen, was tiny and safe. We were supposed to be protected here. And, for the most part we were. But comfort was the enemy. It's when you feel the safest that you're the most vulnerable.

We'd learned that before. In our complacency, we realized evil lurks in the safe places, too.

The quiet places.

The moments of comfort.

The places you feel like nothing could ever harm you.

It waits. It watches. And, eventually, like it or not, it comes for you.

Knowing that, knowing that danger lurks everywhere and we could no longer let our guard down, everything had changed for me. Now, whenever he went out into the world, I felt like I was holding my breath every moment until he returned to me.

Once the coffee pot had brewed enough to fill a mug, I poured myself one, adding in a healthy amount of creamer and a dash of sugar, then sat at the island staring into space.

The house was silent, except for the steady *tick, tick, tick* of the clock on the wall. I watched the steam billow out of my mug, stirring the caramel-colored concoction mindlessly.

A noise came from across the room, and I looked up, forcing a smile when Caroline walked into the room, an oversized T-shirt hanging down to her thighs, her chestnut hair in a messy ponytail atop her head. Sometimes, it still surprised me to realize we had a teenager. There were days, moments really, when she rounded the corner and I still expected to see a girl half her height with chubby cheeks and bangs, rather than the young woman before me. When had that happened? Why did they grow up so fast?

"What's going on?" she croaked, her voice coated with sleep.

I didn't want to worry her. "Your dad was called to a crash. Nothing to worry about. I tried to be quiet. Did I wake you?"

She sank down on the barstool next to me. "I'm not sure. I woke up and was going to get a drink of water in the bathroom when I saw the light on down here."

"I'm sorry, sweetheart. You can go back to bed if you wa—"

We were interrupted as my phone's screen lit up on the island, the shrill ring echoing through the nearly silent house. I stared at Jude's smiling face staring up at me and lifted it to my ear.

"Hello?"

"Michelle, it's bad—" His voice was shaky and low. In the background, I could hear a siren and several people talking.

I stayed still. Steady. Trying not to let Caroline see the worry I knew must be etched on my face. "Who is it? What happened?"

"It's Stephanie Dupont."

My heart dropped, and I stood, walking from the kitchen quickly. When Caroline began to follow me, I held up a hand to stop her. Once in the living room, I lowered my voice. "No. Please tell me she's going to be okay. The boys just lost their father, they can't lose their mother, too—"

"No, Michelle, listen to me." He shushed me. "She's fine. Stephanie's fine. She was getting off her shift at the bar, and she said she saw a car go into the lake."

Relief hit me about Stephanie, but then new worries came. "I don't understand. Whose car? Did you find someone?"

"No." He cleared his throat and the sounds of the voices grew fainter. He'd walked away from the crowd. "No, not yet. I'm trying to decide how to handle this. I don't see any other way around bringing in divers, but—"

"Divers?" My throat grew dry. "To search the lake?"

"And drones. Visibility's low at this hour, but when daylight comes, we'll have to commence the search. Anything else will look suspicious." He paused, but I knew what he was saying. I was suddenly feeling lightheaded, my vision tunneling. "If they find the car, the search may end. It might be okay."

"They can't, Jude. There has to be another way. You…you have to stop them."

He was silent, but I already knew what he was going to

say when he finally spoke. "There's nothing I can do. This is out of my hands."

"You have to—"

"I need you to listen to me, Michelle. There's nothing. Nothing I can do. We're dealing with something too big for me to handle on my own, and there are already other officers here. Too many people are already involved, and we're not halfway done. The state police will have to be notified. We'll have to call in a diving unit, the aquatic search and rescue. I don't have enough pull to cover this up even if I wanted to."

I tried to think. There had to be something. "You're the sheriff. If you can't do anything, who can? The officers will listen to you—Rodriguez, Parker, Martin... Can't you just talk to them? Can't you say she was tired? That she must be mistaken?"

"Not unless she confirmed what I was saying, and she won't. I tried to talk to her, to get a better understanding of what happened, but she's certain about what she saw. If someone really did go down, I have a duty to find them. No matter what."

"But, if you go through with this, you know what else they'll find," I whispered, my voice the lowest it had been.

"I know," he said solemnly. "I don't have any choice. There's nothing tying us to—" He cut off then, and with his voice muffled, hand over the speaker, he called, "Be right there." When his attention was back to me, his voice clear and crisp, he said, "Listen, I've got to go. I'll call when I can."

"What am I supposed to do?" I asked, cool tears lining my eyes.

"Nothing to do," he said, his voice stiff and cold as he fought back against the fear I knew he must be feeling. "Just stay calm. I'll call soon. I love you."

"I love you too," I whispered, my voice trembling so hard it was impossible to discern what I was saying.

I lowered the phone from my ear in time to hear, "Mom?"

When I spun around, Caroline was waiting there, waiting for answers I couldn't give her. Answers that would ruin everything.

What were we going to do?

What the police found at the bottom of our community's private lake, Lake Guinevere, would reveal the secret capable of destroying everything I knew and loved.

What could I do?

CHAPTER TWO

ENZO

"Rivera," I called as I jogged across the soggy riverbank, one hand held above my head to prevent the rain from hitting me in the face, though it was doing a poor job. Flashing squad car lights blinded me as I went. Jude turned his head in my direction at the sound of his surname.

I watched the recognition wash over his face as he turned toward me, pulling the rain jacket farther around his head. He shouted above the noise of the storm, "Mr. Mayor, I didn't expect to see you out here so late." I couldn't help grinning at the professionalism in his tone. Ordinarily, he only called me *Mr. Mayor* as a joke, but Sheriff Jude was almost a caricature of my friend.

"The town's buzzing," I grumbled, running a hand through my sopping hair. "I had seventeen calls before three this morning. What's going on down here? I heard something about Stephanie?"

His jaw tightened, and he jutted his chin toward the river. "Yeah, Stephanie said she saw a car going into the lake when she was driving home."

"Oh, wow…" I turned to look out at the lake slowly,

working to keep my face still, unbothered. "What kind of car?"

"She couldn't identify it," he said. "She just caught a glimpse of taillights before it sank. Said it all happened pretty fast."

"Oh my… Have they been able to recover the car? Figure out who it was? Anyone we know?"

His expression was grim as he swiped a hand across his forehead. "I'm afraid not. Visibility is low anyway, but we'll have to wait for daylight if we have any hope of the divers recovering the car of the…" He trailed off, but there was no need to finish the sentence. I glanced toward the dark water, the storm causing it to lap at the bank with wild vengeance.

I glanced toward the highway several feet to my right, where an officer named Parker could be seen in a neon vest, standing near the squad cars in order to direct traffic, should any make an appearance.

At this time of night, after Bunny's Bar had already closed down, it was unlikely. It stood to reason that whoever had crashed into the lake had to have either been a patron of the bar or an employee. No one else would've been on this side of town this late. All our roads were dead ends, we connected to nowhere, and the bar was the only business we had. Everything else was across the bridge.

"Are there any skid marks? Any reports of other witnesses? Signs of the crash?"

"No," Jude said as lightning flashed overhead. He didn't flinch when I did, already adjusted to the noise of the storm. "Nothing. Rodriguez and O'Hara went down to talk to Bunny and compare her list to the one we got from Stephanie regarding who was still at the bar when they closed. Hopefully we can narrow down who would've had cause to be on this stretch of road so late."

If they hadn't been a patron of the bar or an employee,

they had to have been someone from one of the two subdivisions on this side of the lake.

I nodded, wiping rain from my eyes. "Do you have someone checking our neighborhood? Making sure everyone's home safe?"

"We'll be checking both Southwest and Northwest Acres first thing in the morning. I hardly think it's wise to wake the neighborhood with news we don't have," he said. "We're going to cross-check the lists first and start with those people. We'll move on from there once morning comes."

"I suppose that's when you'll be bringing in the divers."

He nodded. "They're coming from the state. I haven't had a chance to call them yet. We're still securing everything, but that's next on my to-do list." He paused, his expression odd. "Somehow, I just kept hoping she was going to call and say she saw it wrong. This is such a mess."

My heart rate increased, and I swallowed, adjusting in place as I tried to think on my feet. I saw my in and I had to take it. "I mean, do we know for a fact that she saw it? She was tired. She's been doing so much anyway and she'd been working late, so isn't it possible she *did* see it wrong?"

It was a long shot, I knew. In all likelihood, he was going to tell me he was only joking and that, of course, she knew what she saw. I waited impatiently as he hesitated, studying my face. Then, he nodded slowly, almost as if he knew why I was asking.

But he didn't.

Couldn't.

"It's possible, I suppose. I was thinking the same thing for all of those reasons. I mean, it *is* late, and from the highway, she could've just seen a flash of light and thought it was a car. From the statement she gave, it all seemed to have happened fast. If she was mistaken, she's probably too embarrassed to tell us."

"Maybe I should talk to her again before we go getting divers in the water and the state involved. Stephanie's been through so much recently. I'd hate to think this could all just be a misunderstanding."

Much to my surprise, he nodded again. "Yeah, you're right."

"Where's she at?"

"Back at home, but I should go with you."

"You don't have to—"

"No, I know I don't, but with the investigation ongoing, it wouldn't look right for a civilian to be talking to her alone right now. With the state involved, I just want to keep everything on the up-and-up, ya know? It's just easier if we dot all our i's and cross all our t's. You're welcome to come with me, though, if you want. Or I can do it alone."

"No, I'll go." I nodded, already jogging across the muddy ground toward his squad car and sliding inside as he walked toward Parker, saying something to him as he pointed to the lake. The only two other officers, Dessen and Stewart, hurried over to listen to whatever he was telling them. There were several head nods, several eyes fell on the car where I sat, though it was dark and I knew they couldn't see me well, and then Jude hurried my way.

I couldn't believe he was actually going along with it, that it had been so easy, and that I actually might be able to figure my way out of this.

Somehow, I had to.

If not, if they did send divers down to the bottom of our little Lake Guinevere, just seven acres wide and twenty feet deep at her lowest point, I knew what they'd find.

I couldn't let that happen.

CHAPTER THREE

STEPHANIE

The sound of a knock on the door caused me to jump, nearly knocking over the glass of sweet tea in front of me. I stood from the kitchen island and made my way toward the front door, looking outside with apprehension.

When I saw two familiar faces looking in on me, I shuddered, moving the curtains back and pulling open the door.

"Jude? Enzo? What's going on?"

It was Enzo who spoke first, a dark five o'clock shadow on his dimpled chin. "We wanted to talk to you again about what you saw down by the lake."

"The car? Why? Did you find it?" I asked, looking at my neighbors strangely. Had they even had enough time to search? Somehow, I'd expected things to take several days.

"Do you mind if we come inside?" Jude asked as thunder rumbled overhead. I stepped back, allowing them inside, water from their clothes dripping onto the hardwood floor.

Enzo shook, as if he were a dog, while Jude took his coat off carefully, trying to keep the drops on the welcome mat that read "I hope you brought wine."

Ted hated that stupid doormat, but I'd fought with him

over keeping it. He'd said it sounded childish, but I'd argued that children couldn't drink wine. Besides, they were popular, I'd seen them all over my Instagram feed, and what did it really matter? *His* friends weren't judging our doormat like the women in the neighborhood would. In the end, I'd won and now, none of it mattered. I could decorate the entire house with them now and no one would care.

"I tried to text you on the way over to give you a heads-up we were coming," Enzo said, trying to get me to meet his eye. I couldn't do it. I was embarrassed by what I'd done. Terrified I'd be found out. "We were worried you'd be asleep."

"No, I couldn't sleep after what I saw," I said, wrapping my arms around myself. "My phone's charging on the counter. I didn't hear it go off. Sorry."

He nodded slowly, as if he didn't believe me.

Why shouldn't he believe me? As far as they knew, I had no reason to lie. I forced the thought out of my head. "So, the car? You found something?"

"Actually, no," Jude said, hanging his jacket on an empty hook by the door. "We haven't been able to conduct a search yet. We're keeping people away from the area while we wait for the state police to arrive. Before they do, we wanted to ask you if you could recount your story for us again."

"Why?" I felt a shiver run down my spine. What did they know?

"Well, we know it was late," Enzo cut in, his tone somehow light and pointed at the same time. "We just wanted to make sure you saw what you *think* you saw."

"I saw a car," I reaffirmed. It was too late to say anything different now.

"I know you *think* you saw a car, but how could you be su—"

Jude cut him off with a sideways glance. "Look, let me just say this, *if* you saw a car, we're glad you told us. I don't want to make it seem like we're doubting you. It's just that sometimes things can come back to you more clearly after the heat of the moment has passed. If you'd seen a flash of light or a reflection on your window and thought it was a car, but then, after further contemplation, realized it may not have been, I wouldn't want you to feel like you couldn't tell us. It would be an honest mistake. I don't want you to be afraid to tell us because you're worried you'll get into trouble."

"Funny, it sounds like you *are* doubting me, Jude," I said, my bottom lip quivering as I turned to look at Enzo. "Both of you."

"Well, for one thing, there are no tire tracks in the mud, so it makes me question—"

"I told you, it looked like they could've gone down the boat ramp."

Jude nodded seriously, his dark brows drawn down. "I know you did. And you could be right. We just want you to be sure before we ask the state police to come and divers to search for something that isn't there."

I stared at him, running through what he was saying. Why didn't they believe me? Why were they so sure I hadn't seen anything? Was I so easy to read? Did they sense that I was hiding something?

"How long was your shift today?" Enzo asked, his dark cognac eyes drilling into mine.

"I worked at dispatch this morning and then at the bar tonight. Same as usual, so, seventeen-ish hours. That's average for me, though."

"I get that it's usual, but it's also a really long day, and you've been doing it for a while now. Do you think it's possible you were just tired? It's understandable if it's starting to wear on you. Maybe you saw something like Jude said, something that may have looked like a car but probably wasn't?"

"Why are you asking me this?" I demanded, panic settling into my stomach. Why didn't they believe me? What was happening?

"It's just a big deal to have to bring the dive team in and the search and rescue people and the state police," Enzo said, looking at Jude, who nodded somewhat apprehensively. "You know, serious stuff, and it wouldn't look good on any of us if they weren't able to find anything. You need to be really sure about what you saw and exactly where it was, you know? We want to be sure we're sending them down there to look for something." There was a dark twinkle in his eye, as if he were trying to communicate something with me I wasn't truly understanding.

"I saw taillights, just like I told Henry earlier when I called it in."

Enzo was relentless. "But you couldn't make out what kind of car it was? Or even that it was a car at all? Could it have been a truck? An SUV?"

"I…" I trailed off, trying to recall what I'd told the police in my statement. "I don't know. It all happened so fast." I folded my arms across my chest, taking a half step forward defiantly. "Why are you questioning me like I'm a criminal? Matter of fact, why are *you* questioning me at all? Is this what happens when someone reports a crime these days, Jude? The police treat them like they're a suspect? You get the mayor involved to come around and harass them? Is that what it's come to? No wonder people keep their noses in their own business anymore."

"No," Jude said finally, his expression defeated. "No. I'm sorry if it feels that way to you. We're not trying to make you feel uncomfortable or like we suspect you of lying. We don't. Enzo and I are here more as friends than anything. We wanted to check in on you. You know, just want to make sure you're still doing okay after what happened. Make sure that you haven't remembered anything else or found some clarity since we last spoke. I know you've been going through a lot, and—"

My vision clouded with sudden tears. "You mean the fact that my husband disappeared into thin air?" My voice cracked as I opened my mouth again. "Y-yeah, you could say I've been going through a lot."

His eyes were softer then, sympathetic to my hardships. "Exactly. Ted's disappearance has been hard on us all, you more than anyone, of course, and I just..." He leaned forward, as if he were going to tell me a secret. "I know you're trying to help your boys get through this, you're trying to keep everything and everyone above water, and you've all been at the center of the investigation and the media reports and everything. I'm just saying it would be understandable if exhaustion got the best of you. And, being the only witness, you'll be called in for questioning quite a bit. I know how hard that was on you last time. If something criminal were going on, you could be called to testify. I'm not trying to sway you either way. I want you to feel comfortable telling us what you saw, I'm just trying to protect you from the media circus that is sure to come from this. Especially after what you all went through when Ted disappeared."

"I...I hadn't thought of it like that." That was the truth. When I'd reported seeing the car, I'd thought the one conversation with Henry Rodriguez, the officer who'd taken the call, would be the end of it. I never dreamed that I'd be dragging the boys back into the nightmare of interviews and questioning we'd all endured over the past few months. Things had only just begun to calm down. Did I want to subject them to that again?

"Yeah, and, you know, of course we want everyone to be safe, but it's just really easy to see something by mistake and then realize later it wasn't what you saw at all. Do you think that's what may have happened or…" Jude trailed off, watching me. How did he know I was lying? Could he sense it? Why wasn't he more mad? I'd wasted his time. Woken him out of bed, most likely.

I chewed my bottom lip, sweat gathering at my hairline. How was I going to get away with backtracking now? Wouldn't that look suspicious? I needed to stick to my story, didn't I? "Maybe."

To my surprise, both men's eyes lit up, their smiles wide.

"Yeah?" Jude asked.

"Yeah. I mean, I did see something…" I looked away, trying to piece together my thoughts. "But maybe it wasn't taillights, after all. Maybe it was just a flash of light somewhere or a light from a boat sailing across the lake. It all happened so fast, and I *was* tired. I am tired. It's been a long few months. I'm dealing with so much."

"Of course you are," Enzo said, reaching his hand out and resting it on my shoulder. "And of course you're tired. That's to be expected."

My body slumped, the weight of what I'd done resting on me. Why had I ever thought this was a good idea? "Oh, I feel so stupid now. Am I going to be in trouble? I've woken everyone up, caused so much chaos…"

Jude shook his head before I'd even finished with the question. "No, no, no. I don't want you to worry about any of that. Let me take care of everything. Most people don't even know anything happened and, the ones who do, we'll just tell them that upon further reflection, you've realized what you thought you saw wasn't what you actually saw at all. It happens all the time. No one will blame you."

There was a hint of something in both their eyes that sent chills down my spine. Suddenly, a new thought occurred to me. What if they didn't know I'd been lying? If that was the case, why didn't they want the lake searched? What did they know? What were *they* hiding?

Whatever it was, I wanted them out of my house. It was late and the boys were asleep. In a town this small, it was almost impossible not to know your neighbors exceptionally well—their history, their life story, their families, what age they had braces, what they'd worn to our high school prom. These men were no exception. Jude and Enzo were my friends, my neighbors, boys I'd gone to school with. Our children had grown up together, and ordinarily, I'd tell you I would've trusted them with my life, but staring at them that night, it was as if they were strangers.

I was probably being ridiculous. I knew them both so well…at least, I *thought* I did. Now, though, I couldn't be sure.

What I knew was that they were hiding something. Something big.

Lake Guinevere held so many secrets for us all.

How had I not realized that until just then?

"Okay, thank you." I feigned a yawn, hoping they'd take the hint.

"We should let you get some rest," Jude said, his step lighter as he turned around, grabbing his jacket and pulling it back on.

Enzo squeezed my shoulder lightly once more, holding eye contact for an extra second before he pulled away. "Take care of yourself, Stephanie."

I nodded, my voice frozen in my throat as I saw them out, then shut and dead-bolted the door. I watched through the window until the headlights disappeared from my driveway, letting out my first easy breath as they pulled away.

Had Enzo's last sentence been a sign of well wishes? Or a warning?

It was ridiculous, but somehow, it felt like the latter.

CHAPTER FOUR

MICHELLE

The sound of keys in the front door roused me from the sort of half awake, half asleep state I'd been in for more than an hour. It wasn't restful, but my body knew I needed whatever rest I could get. I opened my eyes, sitting up straighter on the sofa. Caroline was asleep next to me, her feet resting on my lap, head at the other end. I eased her feet off of me carefully before standing, just in time to see Jude walk into the room.

"Hey," I said, my heart fluttering as I searched his face for any sort of emotion I recognized. "What happened? Did they find…anything?"

He slipped out of his wet jacket, dropping it and his keys onto the side table and looking over at Caroline. "She's asleep," I assured him. "Has been for a while."

He shook his head finally, keeping his voice low. "They're not going to be searching. It was all a misunderstanding."

"A misunderstanding? What do you mean?"

He walked past me and to the left, heading into the kitchen and opening the refrigerator to pull out a can of soda. "Stephanie changed her statement. She was tired and said she realized it wasn't a car that she saw after all."

What? It seemed too good to be true. "Can she…do that?"

"She already has."

"And it's that simple? It's just… I mean, it's over?" I put a hand to my chest, hesitant to feel the relief that had begun to overwhelm me.

His smile was small and he leaned forward, pressing his lips to my cheek. "I think so, yeah. She retracted her statement. There's nothing else to investigate. She claims it was just a light across the lake that she saw."

I paused. "Did you have something to do with her changing her mind? You didn't tell her anything, did you? Or pressure her? That would be worse, Jude. If she tells anyone—"

"No," he said quickly. "Of course not. You know I wouldn't. Enzo and I went to talk to her, asked her a few questions, and her story began to fall apart."

"Enzo? Why was Enzo there?"

"He came by to see what was going on…" He studied me, looking perplexed. "I thought you'd be happy."

"No, I am. It's just… Well, why would she change her story? It doesn't make sense. I'm glad she did, don't get me wrong, but don't you worry about her suddenly being interested in the lake? What if she changes her story again?"

"She won't. Trust me, it's handled." He kissed my cheek again and walked past me, heading for the stairs. "Now, I need to get out of these clothes and go back to bed." As if to prove his point, he yawned loudly.

I watched him disappear upstairs, a lump forming in my belly. He seemed all too content to believe our problems were behind us, but what had happened opened a whole new sense of fear in me. If this had happened once, it could happen again.

What had Stephanie seen, after all?

What had changed her mind?

I walked across the room and looked out the window. At the front of the subdivision, I could see lights on in both Stephanie's and Enzo's homes, sitting across from each other like bookends to the opening of our cul-de-sac.

What secrets did they know? How close had we come to being found out? How long did we have until our secret was unearthed?

CHAPTER FIVE

ENZO

Once Jude had been home long enough to go upstairs and fall asleep, I walked out of my house, sneaking across the edge of the tree line so my moves would be hidden in the shadows.

I felt like a teenager again, sneaking out of my bedroom window to meet whatever girl I was dating that week. But there was no girl I was after that night. It was a woman.

A woman who'd been avoiding me for months.

After checking both ways, I darted across the grassy circle in the center of our subdivision and into the tree line of Stephanie's yard. I moved forward, toward her door. The light was on downstairs, and I knew she was awake.

How could she not be?

I approached her back door and rapped my knuckles against the wood. I could've called, but she wouldn't answer. She never did anymore.

When the door swung open a few minutes later, her expression morphed from concerned to confused to angry.

"What are you doing here, Enzo?"

"I wanted to talk to you. *Alone.* Can I come inside?"

"The boys are upstairs," she said, not budging. "It's late. I was just getting ready to head up to bed."

"I won't bother them, and I won't stay long. Just give me a few minutes." I cocked my head to the side, hoping to find the softness in her eyes that had once been there. I knew she'd been through a lot and I was trying to respect that, but there was no reason for the coldness she'd met me with lately. "Please."

She huffed out an exhausted breath and stepped back, allowing me to step into the hallway between the laundry room and the garage. "I have to wake up early to make sure the boys get up for school, so whatever it is, let's just get on with it."

I shoved my hands into my pockets, trying to get my head together. Before I'd come, I'd rehearsed what I wanted to say, but now, it all seemed to elude me.

When she moved past me, leading us into the kitchen, I caught the familiar scent of cigarette smoke and fried food on her clothes. *Eau de Bunny's Bar.* I'd smelled it many times on myself or others, but never on Stephanie. After Ted disappeared, she'd had no choice but to find a second job to supplement her income and support the boys. But still, the stench didn't fit her. She wasn't meant to be working in a dank bar all hours of the night. But she'd never listen to me on the matter.

She rested against the edge of the black, granite-topped island, watching me closely. "Well, what is it you want to talk about?"

"I wanted to check in on you, that's all. It's been a while since we've talked. *Really* talked. I know you have a lot going on, but... I mean, is there anything I can do for you? As a friend?" I lowered my voice. "I miss you."

"Enzo, we can't. We've talked about this." Her voice was low and cutting, as if I'd made a mistake by coming there.

24

Maybe I had, but I had to take a chance. I couldn't keep this in any longer. I had too much to tell her.

"I know we have. When Ted first left, I understood why you wanted me to stay away. I did. But it's been four months now. How long are you going to keep pushing me away?"

"My husband is missing," she said through gritted teeth. "Maybe dead. What do you want me to do? Just jump back into everything like nothing ever happened? What we did was wrong. If anyone were to ever find out, they'd hate me. It would destroy the shred of a reputation I'm barely hanging on to."

"No one would hate you," I said quickly, my stomach tightening at the thought. "How could anyone hate you? We wouldn't have to tell them when it started. We could say it's new, that it just happened."

She turned away from me, filling a glass with water from the tap and taking a drink. "I just need more time."

"I understand. I'm not expecting anything. I just want to be here for you. I can't imagine how alone you must feel right now."

"Can't you?" she asked, one brow raised. Truth was, I knew better than most.

"It was different with Leslie. I didn't have a family to keep going when she died. I didn't have to keep us afloat. I got to feel my grief and, as I recall, it was you who was there for me when I was at my lowest point. I'm just trying to repay the favor." I stepped forward, outstretching my hand cautiously. Surprisingly, she didn't stop me, just closed her eyes and leaned her face into my palm.

For a moment, just that moment, I remembered who we'd been. How much I'd cared for her. How much she'd loved me in return.

Then, all at once, she pulled away from me, her body tensing as she put her guard back up.

"I'm sorry, Enzo, I just can't right now. I appreciate you coming over." She met my eyes, holding my gaze for a second longer. "Truly. And we do need to have this conversation, but not tonight. Tonight, I only want to go to sleep. The boys will need to be up in just a few hours, and I'm exhausted."

I nodded, stepping back and withdrawing my hand. "I understand. Just…just promise me that you know I'm here. Whenever you're ready to talk."

"I do. I know." She nodded affirmatively and turned ever so slightly toward the hall. More accurately, the door. I was being dismissed.

I didn't need further coaxing. I was used to being eschewed by her. Ever since her husband's disappearance, she'd pushed me further and further away, avoiding me at every turn. She wanted to keep up appearances, to make it so she could play the role of heartbroken wife, and she'd played it well. Even to me.

If I didn't know any better, I'd believe she truly was grieving his loss.

Of course, I did know better.

I just had to wait it out until she was done with the charade.

CHAPTER SIX

STEPHANIE

When my phone went off the next morning in the middle of preparing dinner for the boys—something easy for them to reheat while I was at work later in the day—I felt a pit growing in my stomach. Something was wrong. Something had happened.

I answered the call, worry plaguing me.

"Hello?"

"Ms. Dupont?"

"Yes."

"This is Britta, from Cason County High. I'm calling because Principal Warner wanted me to touch base with you. We've had a bit of trouble with Rafael today…"

"Trouble? What kind of trouble? Is he hurt?" I switched off the stovetop, moving the skillet of hash brown casserole from the burner.

"No, no he's not hurt. Nothing like that. I, well, I was just supposed to ask if you could come down for a meeting with Principal Warner. I believe she wants to discuss it all with you in person."

I was already making my way through the house, so I

called out a breathless, "Yes, of course. I'm on my way," and ended the call, scooping up the keys to my yellow Jeep as I rushed out the door.

On the way to the school—a route that took me across the lake, while I tried not to think about the events that had recently transpired, then through downtown, and fifteen miles north—I thought of what Raf could've possibly gotten into.

Had he spoken out in class? Had he gotten into a fight? Had he used foul language?

None of it would surprise me, frankly. At one time, my boys had both been sweet, cuddly toddlers, then sweet but less cuddly children. As teenagers, I'd lost sight of the kind, gentle boys they'd once been. It seemed as though lately my days were spent fighting back against the ruffians they seemed determined to become.

When Ted and I had found out we were expecting twins seventeen years ago, my husband had been excited. I'd been terrified. I'd thought then that surviving through the late nights and the potty training and the terrible twos would be the worst of it, but those struggles had been nothing compared to the stress of sharing a home with—and trying to raise—two hormone-controlled young men now.

Add that to the fact that I was parenting totally on my own now and rarely home between my stressful day job and my new night job—both of which combined still *barely* made ends meet—and you could start to understand why I was barely grasping at straws most days.

My boys seemed determined to pull the final straws from me at every turn.

Things had never been easy, but they'd been easier when Ted was still here. When I wasn't doing everything entirely on my own.

Of course, there was Enzo, but that was different. He

couldn't be here for me anymore, not like he was once. Everything had changed with Ted's disappearance. *I* had changed.

As I pulled into the school's parking lot, I took a deep breath, swearing to myself that whatever they'd done, I could handle it. It was hard. It was all just hard. Everything. Everyday. Last year, I would've been going into this meeting with a partner; I would've had someone to help me through whatever was coming. If there was one thing I could count on Ted for, it was making everything look put together, seem okay, even when it wasn't. But, since he left—*disappeared*—everything was different. It was all on me to hold it together—or, at least, pretend I could.

I approached the front door, reading over the warning signs that let me know no weapons were allowed and that all visitors must report straight to the office, and pressed the button.

Over the intercom, the voice I'd spoken to on the phone earlier said, "May I help you?"

"Yes, I'm Dominic and Rafael Dupont's mother. Stephanie Dupont. I have a meeting with Principal Warner." I tucked a piece of my hair behind my ear as the wind picked up, hoping I at least looked somewhat put together, though I'd yet to get ready for work or put on makeup.

There was a brief pause, and then I heard, "It's open."

I pulled on the door and stepped inside the building. There were signs directing me toward the principal's office, though I knew my way from my own time there.

When I walked in the office, Raf was sitting in one of the plastic chairs across from a small, metal desk. The woman behind the desk looked to be not much older than my sons, with a nameplate in front of her that read: Britta Regan, School Secretary. When I walked into the room, she smiled, standing up. "Hello, Ms. Dupont. I've let Principal Warner know you're here. She should be out in—" Her words were interrupted by the opening of a door to my right.

"Ms. Dupont," Leilani Warner said with a stiff nod. We'd gone to school together, just two years separating us, so to pretend now that we were practically strangers for the sake of disciplining my son felt odd at best. "Rafael. Come on in."

Raf hurried past me, shrugging away from my hand as I placed it on his shoulder. We made our way into the small, cramped office and waited as she took a seat.

"So, what's going on?" I finally asked, the question directed at my son. I felt uneasy being the only person in the room without the knowledge of what had happened. His neck was pink with embarrassment, and I'd noticed him avoiding my eye contact at all costs. Whatever had happened, it wasn't good.

Principal Warner folded her hands in front of her, taking a deep breath. "Well, there's no better way to do this, so I'm just going to come right out with it." My stomach flipped and I waited on pins and needles, my skin ice cold. "Your son was caught having sex in Coach Ryan's office during first period."

"He was…" I was breathless, trying to process the sentence. *No.* I wasn't foolish enough to believe my son was a saint, but he wasn't stupid. He wouldn't do something so… My gaze trailed to him, and he'd covered his face with his hands. "Raf, why would you do that? I'm so sorry," I added, directing the apology to Principal Warner. Somehow it made it worse that I knew her so well. What must she think of my parenting, or, apparently, lack thereof? With Ted gone, I'm sure they all thought I'd lost my grip on the boys, that their father was the only thing that had kept us together for years. I stared at my son, anger and embarrassment radiating through my body. "Why would you… What were you thinking?"

He groaned loudly, rolling his eyes. "I don't know. We've

all established it was wrong and I got caught. Can we just get on with the punishment already? This is mortifying."

"Yeah, well, it should be mortifying, Rafael. What you did is inexcusable. You know better. Your father and I raised—"

"Dad's not here anymore, Mom. So why don't we all just move on with our lives?" He stood, moving past me in anger.

"Sit down, Mr. Dupont."

"Bite me." He nipped his teeth toward her angrily.

"*Rafael*, are you kidding me? You don't speak to Principal Warner, to any adult that—" He cut me off by walking out of the room and slamming the door. Now it was my turn for my cheeks to flame red with embarrassment. I turned around to face Leilani. "I'm so sorry. I don't know what's gotten into him lately. I really don't. Since his dad..."

She held up a hand, cutting me off. "I know you're all going through a rough time since Ted's..." She paused, seeming to decide which word to use. In truth, everyone— myself included—assumed Ted was either dead or had run off with another woman. I never knew who was in which camp. Perhaps T-shirts were in order... "Disappearance," she landed on. Safe. Simple. "And we've tried to go easy on the boys because of that, but Stephanie, it's not the first time."

"Not the first time he—"

"Sorry, no," she said quickly. "I mean, it is *definitely* the first time we've caught him doing *this,* but it's not the first time we've had trouble out of him. *Them,* really. Both boys have always had a bit of a wild streak, but it was always simple things. Acting out in class, skipping certain periods, pranks on classmates, and the usual teen stuff... But since Ted, it's all changed. We've lost control of them. Their behavior is worse. Darker. More unpredictable. They've both begun skipping entire days. They're cursing in class, yelling at their teachers. Last week, Dominic kicked over his desk after a disagreement with Ms. McDonald, Rafael has been accused of writing several profanities on the walls of the boys' bathroom. I'm afraid if we don't get to the bottom of it now, we may never."

"I don't understand… I had no idea any of this was going on. Why am I just now being told this is happening?"

She grimaced. "I was trying to protect you. Deep down, I've always believed the boys are good kids, and I know what losing their father must be doing to them. I know how much you've got on your shoulders now, too. I wanted to help you as much as I could, take some of the stress on myself rather than involve you. I've talked to the boys, tried to make them understand how serious their actions have been. I really thought it was just a phase for them. That, after a month or two, things would calm down. But we're going on four months now, and they're only getting worse. Their grief has turned to rage, and they're taking it out on their classmates and teachers. I'm sorry, Stephanie, I want to make it work, but if we can't get them under control, I'm going to have no choice but to expel them both."

"Expel?" I put my hand over my stomach, my world spinning. "I… The nearest school is a county over. This place is their home. It's all they've ever known. If you expel them, what would we do? What am I supposed to do with them?"

"Well, there's always homeschooling. The boys only have a year left."

I shook my head, tears welling in my eyes. I couldn't homeschool them and work two jobs, I just couldn't. Just the thought of it made me even more tired than I already felt. But letting either of my jobs go wasn't an option. We'd be broke and out on the street within a few months. And there was no way I could trust them to homeschool themselves. They'd dart out the door the first chance they got and never bother to do any of the work.

No, that just couldn't happen. Sensing my panic, Leilani

leaned forward. "Now, hey, I don't want you to worry right now. We're not to that point yet. That's why I've had you come in today. Hopefully this intervention will help bring reality into perspective for the boys." She paused, then added with a lighter, more cautious tone, "I also wanted to mention, perhaps you could try therapy for them. It might help for them to have someone to talk to about everything."

I scoffed, dabbing the corner of my eye with a tissue from the box on her desk. "I can't even get them to talk to me. There's no way they'd talk to a therapist."

"You never know. Most of the time, when we start seeing this sort of behavior, it's the beginning of an even bigger cry for help. We just have to find the way that the boys need to be communicated with so we can head off any sort of disaster."

"I'll…see what I can do," I said finally. "What about today? Can he stay or does he need to leave? What about the girl's parents?"

"I'm going to be having a meeting with them as well. We've suspended them both for the rest of the day over the incident. Luckily it was Coach and not a student who found them, and I think their embarrassment is punishing them both quite a bit, but if there's a next time, we're going to have to look at more serious punishments," she said firmly, nodding her head slowly as if to be sure I understood.

"There won't be a next time. I'll talk to him. I'll talk to them both."

"Thank you. Dominic can stay, obviously. But I'm giving you the warning about them both. I'll work with you as much as I can. Tonya's always on staff to help counsel the boys, but we can only do so much."

"I understand." I stood, patting her desk. "Thank you, and I'm genuinely so sorry about this."

She smiled, but it was sad. "It's not your fault, Stephanie.

None of this is your fault. Just take care of yourself, okay? And the boys. We'll get this all figured out."

I nodded. "I'll talk to him. I promise this won't happen again."

I started to move for the door, but she stopped me by speaking again. "Oh, Stephanie?"

I winced. What else could there possibly be? "Yeah?"

"I wanted to remind you about the memorial for Ted."

"Memorial?" The word slammed into my chest. He wasn't dead. How could you have a memorial for someone who wasn't dead?

A confirmation washed over her expression as she pressed her lips together. "The boys didn't mention it to you."

I shook my head. "No, they didn't."

"Well, that's okay. It all sort of fell together at the last minute. I asked them to tell you last week, but we're putting together a service for him," she said. "I thought it would be nice, for his birthday, you know. Some of the community members, the parents, have been asking me for it, and that seems like the perfect time. It will just be something small, we'll give the students a chance to say something nice about him—a memory, what they miss most, something like that—and I thought it would be really sweet if the boys would speak as well."

"So, you're doing it on his actual birthday? *Tomorrow?*" I'd planned to spend the day avoiding thinking of him at all.

"Yes. I realize it's short notice. As I mentioned, I did tell the boys last week, but I thought since I had you here, I'd go ahead and remind you as well. I guess it's a good thing I did."

"Yeah, they… I'm sure it slipped their minds."

"I'm sure. We've just thrown it together in a matter of days, so I understand if the timing won't work for you. You're so busy lately."

I bristled at her comment. "No, I'll...I'll figure something out."

"Great. I know it would mean a lot to everyone to have you there."

I nodded.

"And you wouldn't need to bring anything, of course. We'll have the PTA handle that. You can just show up and let us help you however we can."

Again, I nodded. "Thanks, Leilani. I'll do what I can to be there."

With that, I was dismissed. I made my way out of the office with a nod toward Britta, then out of the school. In the parking lot, much to my relief, I saw Rafael sitting on the wheel stop in front of an empty parking spot beside our car. His head was hung down, but when he heard me coming, he stood, his body tense. Still, he wouldn't look at me.

We got into the car without a word, and I started it up, pulling out of the parking lot. Once we were out on the road, I began, "So are you going to tell me what you were thinking, Raf?"

He gave a dry laugh, staring out the window with one hand gripping the handle above his head. "I was thinking I wanted to get laid, I guess."

"Don't talk like that," I snapped. "You can't... God, I don't even know where to begin. How could you be so stupid? Do you realize how serious this is? You could be *expelled*, son."

He shrugged one shoulder. "I'm just a stupid guy, Mom. What can I say?"

"You're not stupid." My eyes began watering again. "You're not stupid. Look at me." I tried to meet his eye, but he didn't budge, keeping his gaze on the window. I reached over, grabbing for his chin to pull him to look my way, but he shoved my arm away.

"Get off, Mom. What do you want? I don't have to look at you to hear you."

"You're not stupid. Do you hear me? You're not," I repeated. "You're just grieving. And you're trying to make sense of something that really doesn't make any sense at all. I get that. I do. But you have to talk to me. You have to let me in or you're going to bottle all that hurt up until you explode."

He nodded but didn't respond.

"I should punish you for what you did, but I know you're not a bad kid. I know you're hurt by your dad's disappearance." I paused. "Were you at least safe? When you... I mean..." Now it was me who couldn't look at him.

"Oh my god, Mom. Please don't talk to me about this." He tossed his feet onto the dashboard, sliding down in his seat.

"Well, were you? I know you know about sex, and I don't expect you to be abstinent—"

"My god." He released a long, drawn-out groan.

"But I do expect you to be smart. Condoms, birth control, getting tested... You have to think about all of these things. You do not need a child right now or—"

"Jesus Christ, Mom. I know. Can you just drop it already?"

"If you promise me you're being safe."

"I'll promise you I'll never have sex again if you just drop this fucking conversation."

My body tensed at the word. *"Language!"*

"Dad never cared if I cussed."

"Well, your dad isn't here, is he?" I demanded, feeling the sting of his words. "I am."

"Unfortunately."

Cool tears lined my eyes, and I looked away, trying not to let him see how much the statement had hurt me. The car

constantly being dragged to each other's houses for game nights and dinners, or to tag along to events with our men. When we'd purchased houses in the same subdivision, had children at the same time, I think we both resigned ourselves to the reality that, like it or not, we had to be friends. Or, at least, we had to make everyone believe we were.

Still, I couldn't come straight out and ask her what had happened. I needed the conversation to occur naturally if I wanted any real answers. As I drew nearer to her, I realized she'd been crying. Her cheeks were splotchy and red, her eyes bloodshot. She pressed her lips together, watching me without a word.

"Are you okay?" I repeated.

"What do you want, Michelle?" Her tone was cool. Bitter.

"I-uh, sorry… I didn't mean to bother you. I just saw you out here and thought I'd check in. I didn't realize… I can just go, if you want me to."

She gave a sharp nod, sniffling, and looked away from me, back toward the house. "I'm fine, I'm just in the middle of something."

"Anything I can help with?"

"No. Not really."

"Okay." I took a step back, irritated by her cold demeanor. "Well, if you need anything, I'm around." She folded her arms across her chest, nodding as she began to cry again.

"Thanks," she said quickly, then turned away from me and headed back up her paved driveway and toward her front door. I did the same, turning around, walking through the grassy circle again, and approaching my house.

When I stepped inside, chilled and angry over the strange encounter, I replayed it in my head. Had I done something wrong? Stephanie had never been outright rude to me, not like that.

What exactly had gone on last night? Did more happen

than Jude had let on? Had he upset her somehow? Had he forced her to change her statement?

No. Stop it.

I was being ridiculous.

I knew my husband. I knew what he was capable of, and I knew how much pride he took in being Cason County's sheriff. He wouldn't have done anything to jeopardize that, and if he had, he wouldn't have lied to me about it. At least, I didn't think he would.

We didn't have secrets, not after all we'd gone through.

I moved the curtain covering the window aside, looking back out at Stephanie's house. She hadn't gone inside.

Instead, she'd waited until I'd disappeared into my house before retracing her steps, returning to the edge of the drive and hurrying across in front of the opening of our subdivision.

What the... She was heading...*to Enzo's house?*

Yes. I watched her scurry up the path toward his front door, her arm swinging back as she rapped on it loudly.

What was she doing talking to Enzo? And why was she trying to hide that from me? I couldn't see Enzo, nor the door opening, but I watched her disappear into the house. She was gone.

She'd gone to him.

Why?

An uncomfortable sense of cold sank into my stomach.

Worry. Fear.

What if they knew something?

What if they knew what we'd done?

CHAPTER EIGHT

ENZO

I swung the door open, annoyed by the incessant banging, and my jaw dropped at the sight of Stephanie standing on my front porch. She looked upset, her cheeks blotchy and glistening with tears, her eyes red.

"Hey, uh, let me call you back, Ma." I pulled the phone from my ear before she'd had a chance to respond, and Stephanie stepped into the house without me having to invite her inside.

"What's going on? What's wrong?" My muscles were tense as I waited for an answer. What had happened? Why was she crying? Why was she here?

She sniffled, her arms wrapped around herself as she stifled a sob. Every nerve in my body, every muscle, every cell wanted to reach for her, wanted to gather her in my arms. But, after last night, I had to be stronger than that. She needed to make the first move. "I'm sorry. I didn't know who else to come to."

"Don't apologize. What's going on?" My plan fell apart at once. It was no use. I had no willpower when it came to her. I

43

never had. I tucked my phone into my pocket and pulled her to my chest. "Talk to me."

"It's the boys," she said, swiping her cheek against my shirt, her body curled into mine in a way it hadn't in so long. It felt natural. Normal. She was supposed to be here. With me. I was supposed to be the one she came to when she needed something.

I cleared my throat, rubbing her back with one hand as I tried to run through the possibilities of why she'd be crying. "The boys? What's wrong with them? Are they hurt? Did something happen?"

"No, nothing happened. Well, yes, *some*thing happened. Their father is gone, Enzo. Gone. Something really big happened, and they've just, I don't know. They're lost almost as much as he is, but they're still here with me. They miss him. They miss him so much, and I don't...I can't...I don't know how to keep things running without him."

Oh. Why did that sound like she missed him? Like she wished he were here, rather than me? I stiffened against her, my arms dropping away. "You don't have to do this alone. You know that."

She wiped her eyes, nodding at me slowly. "I do know that. Of course, I do. I'm so grateful for all you've done for me, for you always being there, for...God, for everything. But Ted's disappearance is still too recent for them. I can't move on until we're sure he's not coming home."

"Because him coming home would change the way you feel about me?" Maybe his disappearance already had. She'd never said as much, always using the excuse that people would destroy her if anyone ever found out about us, but I was beginning to worry that was just all too convenient an excuse. After all, in the years before her husband had disappeared, we'd fallen for each other. Hard and fast. We'd planned a future together. A future that didn't involve either of our spouses.

Now, by a twist of fate, that was the exact reality we were faced with, and rather than pulling closer to me, she'd shut me out harder than ever before. For four months now, we'd hardly spoken. So why was she here now? What did she want from me?

"No, Enzo," she said after a moment, but I didn't believe her. Couldn't. "No, it wouldn't change how I feel about you."

"And how is that, exactly? How do you feel about me?" I asked, narrowing my gaze at her.

"Are you seriously going to do this right now?" she demanded. "I came to you crying, dealing with something so serious, and you want to make this about yourself."

"Well, why *did* you come to me? You shut me out of your house yesterday. You shut me out of your life before that. What am I supposed to do? Just sit around and wait for your husband to come back? For you to decide what it is you want? I can't do that anymore. I love you, you know I do, but—"

She put a hand on my chest. "Please don't—"

I brushed it away. I needed to say this, and she needed to hear it. "No, let me finish. I want to be there for you. I want to help you through it. You know I care about Dominic and Rafael, but you have to let me in or let me go. I can't keep waiting in limbo."

"So that's it? No time for me to process all that's happened? Just decide now, all or nothing?" She shrugged helplessly.

"You've had four months, and years before that. You said you loved me, but now you aren't sure. You either want to be with me or you don't. You can't keep using me—"

"*Using you?*" she asked, her eyes wide with outrage. "I

never thought I was using you, Enzo. I was there for you when Leslie died—"

"Exactly. So let me be here for you now."

"That's what I'm trying to do!"

"But only when it's convenient for you!"

We were toe to toe, our faces mere inches apart, our breathing heavy. I was ready for the fight, ready to let her hear all the ways she'd hurt me, all the ways I loved her, but instead, she took a heavy breath and stepped back. She folded her arms across her chest and looked down at the floor. "I'm sorry. I just thought you could help as a friend. I'm… I don't know what I'm doing. I'm so sorry. I know I'm being selfish. I know this isn't fair to you. The boys are really struggling, and their behavior…" She shuddered. "They're getting into trouble at school and causing me issues at home, and I'm just in over my head. I thought… I don't know what I thought." Finally looking up from the floor, she met my eye with desperation. "It's not your problem. I have to figure this out on my own."

"It's not that it's not my problem. It's that it can only be my problem if you'll let it be my problem. Listen, if you want me to help, I'll do whatever I can. I'll talk to the boys. I'll help you around the house. I'll help you with your bills. I'll run errands. I'll help you however you need, Steph. I've always said that. But you have to bring down the walls. I'm not their father. I'm never going to be. And I'm not your boyfriend right now; maybe I never was. You've made that clear. So you can't expect me to come around and help out when you and I are in this weird place. If we're together, fine, I'll do what I can. But if you're still keeping me at arm's length and using me to suit your needs, I deserve better than that. I'm not going to let you jerk me around for much longer."

She whipped her head up to stare at me. "Jerk you

around, Enzo? Really? Is that what you think I've been doing?"

"What else do you call it? You're hot and cold. After all this time of us planning a life together, all this time of you saying you loved me, you haven't said it in months. You'll randomly show up to sleep with me when it suits your needs, but we can't do anything else. No more phone calls, no weekends away, nothing. And, fine, I get it. I'm not heartless. I know what you've gone through, but you and Ted weren't happy. You hadn't been for years. So why, suddenly, are you pretending—to me, to yourself, to everyone—that you're grieving so hard—"

"*He was my husband,*" she whined, stomping her foot. "The father of my children, and he's missing. Losing him is the hardest thing I've ever experienced, and I'm still sitting in a sort of limbo myself because I don't know if he's coming back. I don't know if he left me or if he's with someone else or if something terrible has happened... If you can't understand why I might need some space right now, why I need time to—"

"Time, yes. Fine. But when will it end? What if they never find Ted? What if he does come home? What if he's left for good? You have to decide what it is that you want. It's not fair to me for you to keep putting it off."

"Fair?" She scoffed, tucking a piece of hair behind her ear, her eyes wide. "You're such an ass sometimes, you know that? How can you talk to me about fair? My husband is missing!"

"*And my wife is dead.*" I raised my voice, then when she flinched, lowered it again. "And I grieved her loss. It was one of the most devastating times of my life, but you know what? I turned to you when that happened. You helped me through it. I didn't push you away. I didn't make you question if you still mattered to me. You were always the most important

47

thing to me, Stephanie. Even then. It breaks my heart that you can't say the same."

She looked down, sucking her bottom lip into her mouth. "I have the boys to think about. It's different."

"I get that, but here you are coming to me like I should have a say in what you do with the boys, yet you won't let me be around them. How many times have I asked if you would bring them over for dinner? Or if the four of us could go away for a ball game or concert? Every time you've said no. I'm trying here, but you have to meet me at least some of the way. It doesn't even have to be halfway, but come on, give me an inch here. If you want my advice, want me to play the role of their father, then you have to give me some of the reins."

"You aren't being fair." Her brows knitted together angrily.

"Well, that makes two of us."

She huffed out a defensive breath. "Whatever. I came to you as a friend. I thought you'd be there for me."

"That's just it." I stepped forward, closing the space between us. "I don't want to be your friend, Stephanie. I never have. I love you. I want to be with you, but it's like you said, this is all or nothing for me. I've never misled you to think differently, and I won't start now."

She stared at me, her hazel eyes darting between mine, and then shook her head. "I need to go."

"Right on schedule," I said with a puff of breath from my nose. I kicked off on my heel, turning sideways. This was how it was always going to be with her, wasn't it? Was I just kidding myself to hope for what we'd once had?

She turned away from me, grabbing hold of the door handle and swinging it open without another word. I let her go. There was nothing left to be said between us. I'd made my choice, made my intentions known, and it was up to her to let me know where she stood. I'd done my waiting, played my part, but I wouldn't take another step in her direction until she gave me cause.

I had to respect myself more than that, no matter how badly it hurt.

And, as she walked out the door, slamming it behind her without another look in my direction, I had to hope she'd come to her senses eventually.

If not, what had this all been for?

CHAPTER NINE

STEPHANIE

I slammed the door with all my strength, hoping I knocked a picture or two from his perfect walls as I went. My vision tunneled, my thoughts racing as I hurried across the street to my house.

He was such an ass.

He'd made me feel listened to once.

Loved.

Cared for.

But now, at a time when I needed his understanding more than anything, he'd refused it. He made me feel like I owed him something. Like if I couldn't give him exactly what he wanted, I was no use to him.

There was a time when I'd planned a future with him, loved and wanted to be with him so much I was sure my heart would burst, but those feelings were confused these days, mixed in with guilt, grief, worry, anger, stress, and outright exhaustion.

I'd never known Enzo to be so heartless, but that was how it felt now.

I couldn't for the life of me understand why he couldn't

understand my feelings. Why he was willing to throw it all away, to lose me in every way, if he couldn't have me in the way he wanted. I just needed time, and that was something he wasn't ready to give.

Growing up rich and entitled, the mayor's son and eventually the mayor himself, he could probably count the number of times he'd been told *no* on one hand. Much like Ted, Lorenzo Barone was one of Cason Glen's golden boys, and I'd broken his heart. I wasn't sure he'd ever forgive me.

I froze, staring ahead at the car in the driveway. More accurately, at the person in the car in the driveway. A young girl I didn't recognize sat on Dominic's lap, facing him in the driver's seat, her hair hanging over her face as she kissed him. As I looked closer, I realized she was topless, as was he.

My body went cold.

Seriously?

Out here in public? Out in the driveway with no regard for who sees them or who walks up? I wasn't sure I could handle another confrontation with my hormone-riddled sons—it was as if the universe was enjoying kicking me while I was already down—but I had no choice.

What if someone saw? What would they think? Likely what they already thought. Just another way I was failing.

I hurried forward, pulling at the locked door handle angrily. I pounded on the glass. They jumped, breaking apart at the noise. Dom looked horrified as he recognized me. He pushed the girl off of him, and she grabbed her shirt from the floorboard. I realized she still had on a tiny, nude-colored camisole and her pants, but from the looks of it, she wouldn't have for long.

"Mom?" He slung the door open, adjusting himself in his pants as the girl pulled the top over her head, backward and inside out. Upon closer inspection, she looked oddly familiar. "What the hell? I thought you were at work?"

"And, so what? You thought I was at work so you were just free to do whatever you wanted? Dom, seriously, I don't need this today." I leaned down a bit more so I could see the girl. "Hi, honey, sorry to interrupt, but Dom is now grounded. I'm going to have to take you home."

"*Mom, come on,*" Dom begged. "Chill out. I can take her. You're embarrassing me."

"Go upstairs and wait for me in your room," I said firmly before looking back at the girl. "Where do you live?"

"It's okay," she said, stepping out of the car and adjusting her clothes once more. She refused to meet my eyes, her cheeks bright pink with embarrassment. "I just live down the road. I can walk."

"No, you don't need to—"

"Upstairs, Dom. *Now,*" I snapped, pointing toward the house with a snap of my fingers and interrupting his argument. I turned back around to her as I spoke. "You're from here in Cason Glen, then? I don't mind taking you." I searched the driveway for her, confused for a moment, then realized she'd already jogged down the driveway, phone in hand.

I should've tried to stop her, my instincts said, but I had no patience or time for it. Instead, I followed Dom in the house and up the stairs. I had enough parenting to deal with on my own. I couldn't worry about raising someone else's child.

We marched up the stairs in unison, me just a few steps behind him. "I seriously can't believe you did that. It's like you hate me or something," he said with a scowl, glancing over his shoulder to make sure I saw it.

"I don't hate you, Dom. You know that's not true, but that was not okay."

"Fine, you don't hate me. You just don't want me to have any sort of social life. You're so embarrassing."

"Well, I'm sorry you feel that way, but you know better than to bring a girl home when I'm not here."

"Is that why you're mad? Seriously? It wasn't like we were in my room."

"No, you were making perfect use of your car. We have neighbors. Kids that play on the sidewalk after school. What if someone had been outside? No one needs to see you making out with your little girlfriend in our driveway. And that"—I jutted my thumb over my shoulder though he was no longer looking at me—"was a lot more than just making out."

"*Oh my god.* You're being so dramatic. It was nothing."

"It was *not* nothing." We'd reached the top floor and he spun around to face me.

"Why can't you ever just be cool, Mom? Dad wouldn't have said anything. He never di—" He stopped, cutting himself off.

I cocked my hip, waiting. "What were you going to say?"

"Nothing. Never mind." He pulled his phone out of his pocket, turning away from me.

"No, we are far from done, Dominic Michael. Whatever your dad let you do when I wasn't around was between the two of you, but you're not to have girls here when I'm not home. I know you and your brother think you're grown and you're going to have sex—"

He scowled. "*Ugh*, Mom, please—"

"Don't groan at me. If you're old enough to have it, you're old enough to hear your mom talk about it. I can't stop you from having sex. I know that. But you have to be careful. And safe. You have to—"

"I know what I'm doing," he said firmly. "Stop treating us like little kids. We're not."

"I don't treat you like—"

"What happened?" The door to Rafael's room opened and he stood in the doorway, his gaze darting between us both.

"Go back into your room. I'm talking to your brother."

"Mom caught me with Tuesday."

"Sick." He gave a dark laugh. "What were you doing?"

Dom's brows shot up, a secret answer that seemed to please his brother.

"The girl's name is Tuesday?" I asked, but the conversation no longer seemed to include me at all.

Dom had turned to face his brother, leaving no space for me between my boys. "She's totally freaking out."

"Lame. She's PMSing today. Freaked out on me, too."

Dom snickered. "Heard what you did."

Raf nodded, pride in his expression. "Who from?"

"Everyone's talking about it."

"Sweet."

"Did Coach Ryan really—"

"Yep."

"Fucking legend," he said, holding up his hand to give Rafael a high five.

"*Language*," I called, to which both boys laughed. Dom turned around, moving to walk away from us, and Rafael shut the door without a warning. I looked between them, trying to decide between scolding Rafael again for seeming so proud of what he'd done and dealing with Dom.

Rock, meet hard place.

I hurried across the hall, choosing to deal with the son I hadn't spent the majority of my day scolding and prevented him from shutting the door. "You have to stop this. Both of you."

"Stop what?"

"Stop acting out. Stop getting into trouble at school. Stop bringing random girls to our house. Stop acting like you're an adult when you're not."

"Why do you even care what we do? You're never here! Dad's gone and you're gone, and we had to grow up. Don't you see that? If you would've just kept him happy, he never would've left us."

His words were sharp, slicing me like a knife. I paused, taking a deep breath as I forced away the tears I felt welling in my eyes. "You know this is not my fault."

"Dad couldn't stand living with you, and neither can we. I wish I could disappear, too."

There was no stopping the tears then. They clouded my vision, blurring the sight of my son in front of me. "I'm sorry to hear that, son. I really am. I love you. I love you and your brother, and I'm doing the best I can. Can't you make it easier on me?"

He was unaffected by my tears, pulling out his phone and responding to a message with a smile. "You're making it hard on yourself, Mom. We're grown. Just let us do what we want to do."

I snatched the phone from his grasp. "What? So you can both end up as teenage fathers? So your brother can get expelled? Is that what you want? You're not going to do this. You're not going to throw your life away. Your father and I worked too hard to give you everything for you to squander it by being stupid and making a mistake—"

"I'm not going to get anyone pregnant. We're not stupid." He held out his hand. "Give me my phone."

"You can't know that, son," I said exasperatedly. "Accidents happen every day. I know you're almost grown. I know I can't do anything to stop you from dating, or even having sex, but you have to be safe. You can't bring girls here, you can't have sex at school—"

"So now I'm being punished for something Raf did?"

"You're not being punished—"

"Whatever, Mom. Are you grounding me or what? 'Cause

if not, I have homework." I'd almost forgotten I still had his phone in my hand when he reached out and swiped it from my palm.

"Why won't you talk to me? I'm not being unreasonable here. I'm trying to understand—"

"But you can't understand. You're not a guy. You don't get what it's like."

Now *that* I understood. I heard what he was saying loud and clear. I wasn't their father. I'd never get it. "I'm not a guy," I said slowly. "You're right. But I understand what it's like to have…desires and curiosities and—"

He interrupted me with a gagging noise. "Nope. No. No. I'm not having this discussion with you."

"Dom, please, we need to talk about this—"

"Never in a million years. Get out of my room." He pointed toward the door as if I were a child being sent away.

"Is she your girlfriend or…?"

He scoffed. "*Girlfriend?* Please. What is this, *1990?*"

"I just… She looked familiar, but I couldn't figure out who she was. Is she in your class? You've never talked to me about seeing anyone."

"Don't be weird about this, please. You don't know her. We're just hanging out. It's nothing serious," he said, lowering his hand as his phone buzzed again. He began typing out a new message.

"Well, it looked pretty serious," I said.

"Well, looks can be deceiving."

"Dom, girls have different feelings when we're that age. Sex is a really big deal for—"

"I don't want to talk to you anymore, Mom. Not about this. So either punish me or leave me alone. I'm still pissed that you embarrassed me, and I have homework to do."

"I didn't mean to embarrass you, but you have to learn—"

"To never bring girls here. Got it." He nodded his head. "Won't happen again."

"She deserves more respect than to just be someone you're having fun with—"

"You don't even know her." He scowled. "Just please, Mom, go."

"I know girls like her. I know how it feels to be a teenage girl. You have to know that what you're doing affects her—"

"*Mom*," he begged loudly. "Please. Just...God, just go."

I shook my head, my body trembling with a helpless sort of anger. I was outnumbered. Alone. Embarrassing. My boys were counting down until they didn't have to deal with me anymore. Wishing they could disappear like their father. Or, more likely, wishing I'd been the parent to disappear in the first place. I looked into his soft, brown eyes, wondering when it all changed. There was a time when he'd loved me more than anyone else in the world. When he couldn't wait to wrap me in a sticky hug at the end of a long day. When their worlds revolved around me and Momma could solve everything.

But it would never be that way again.

Without another word, I lowered my head, moving away from him and making my way out of the room. They were turning out more like their father than I'd realized. Was it too late to fix that?

CHAPTER TEN

MICHELLE

When Jude's shift ended and he arrived home, I was finishing up my latest blog post from the couch, curtains thrown back so I could keep an eye on my neighbors.

I'd had a hard time focusing on the task at hand, scraping each word from my brain as if by literal force—erasing and reattempting each paragraph.

When he walked inside, I shut the laptop and placed it on the coffee table.

"Hey."

"Hey." He looked me over, obviously confused. "What are you doing? Working in here today?"

"Yeah, I guess I needed a change of scenery." I scooped up my glass from the side table, melting ice cubes collecting at the bottom, and followed him into the kitchen where he pulled a Diet Coke from the fridge.

"How was your day?"

I hadn't decided what I was going to say to him or how I wanted to approach the subject, but Jude and I didn't have secrets. I needed to be honest with him about my worry.

"It was fine. I had a live stream this morning, and I've been trying to get today's post finalized ever since. I need to nail down next week's schedule, but I've had trouble focusing. How was yours?"

He cracked open the soda and took a drink, expelling a long sigh afterward. "Same old, same old. Trouble focusing? Something on your mind?"

I nodded, placing my glass in the sink and turning around to face him. "Actually, yes. Something strange happened today..."

He'd lifted the drink back to his lips but froze at my words and lowered it again. "What happened?"

"It was Stephanie. I saw her outside. She was...well, she'd *been* crying. She seemed distracted and distant. I approached her to see if there was anything I could do, and..." I trailed off, recalling the incident.

"And?" he pressed on.

"Well, it was just strange. She seemed angry with me, but I thought maybe she was just upset for whatever reason—"

"I'm sure that was the case. You two haven't been having any issues, have you?"

"No. Not that I know of, but when I came back inside, she pretended like she was going back to her house, too. And once I was in the house, when she thought I wasn't watching, she turned around and went to Enzo's."

"Enzo's?" He furrowed his brow. "Weird. What's that about?"

"I don't know, but it felt strange to me. You said he was with you last night when you went to talk to her."

"Yeah, so?" He raised an unconcerned brow.

"So, are you sure you didn't insinuate that you didn't want them to search the lake? Did you say or do anything that might've made them suspect something was up?"

"Of course not." He scoffed.

"Well, what if he figured it out somehow? What if he's suspicious of you? What if she is? What if the two of them are together talking about us? What if they figure out what we did?"

"Stop," he said quickly, placing his soda on the counter and taking a step toward me, his hands resting on my arms. "You're spiraling. I know last night brought back a lot of the worry from before, but nothing's changed. We're safe. They're not searching the lake, and whatever Enzo and Stephanie were doing together, I'm sure it had nothing to do with us or what happened last night."

"What then? Why else would she have been so standoffish? You don't, at least, think it's an odd coincidence?"

"An odd coincidence, sure, but that's all it is," he said, shaking his head. "What else could it be? I didn't let on that I wanted to keep the lake from being checked. I couldn't. I was professional as always. She had no idea I was opposed to the idea at all. If anything, it was Enzo who seemed to want to talk her out of it."

"*Enzo?* Really? Why?"

"I have no idea, but maybe that's what they were talking about today."

"I've never seen them visiting each other's houses before. Not without Leslie or Ted."

He huffed out a breath of air, staring at me dubiously. "Well, we are all friends. It wouldn't be the craziest thing if losing their spouses brought them closer together."

"I guess that's true," I conceded. Then, a strange thought occurred to me. "You don't think it brought them *close* close, do you?"

He laughed. "God, no. There's no way."

He was right. It was a wild accusation. Enzo and Stephanie had nothing in common. Nothing, of course, besides Ted.

"Just relax, okay? You have nothing to worry about. Absolutely nothing. We covered our tracks. We're not going to be caught."

"That's what everyone who's ever gotten caught says," I pointed out.

"Well, what would you like me to do?" he asked, exasperation in his tone. "Do you want me to go over and talk to them? See if they act strangely? Ask them if they suspect that we've done anything wrong?" He was joking. Patronizing me. I shook my head, feeling angry.

"You shouldn't joke about things like that. What if I'm right? What if they do suspect something and you confirmed it last night? What if they're going to try and turn us in?"

"Turn us in to *who*, Michelle?" He kissed my forehead softly. "They'd have to come to me to do that. Trust me, you're getting yourself worked up over nothing." With that, he stretched an arm over his head and walked out of the room. I listened to him moving farther away, up the stairs and overhead, his statements repeating in my mind.

Was he right?

Was I just being paranoid because we'd come so close to being caught last night?

I wanted to think that was the case. That he'd know better than anyone if we were in trouble. There were perks to being married to the county sheriff when you'd done something so terrible, of course, but still, I was struggling with the nagging worry in my stomach.

Something felt wrong to me.

Off.

Unsafe.

I felt as if we were being watched.

As if someone knew our secret.

That wouldn't do at all.

CHAPTER ELEVEN

ENZO

I was drinking a beer when the phone rang a few hours later. I half expected it to be Stephanie but was relieved —*okay, maybe a little disappointed*—to see it was my sister instead.

"Yeah?"

"Enzo, hey, please tell me you've seen Sophie."

"Sophie?" I furrowed my brow. "No, why would I have?"

She sighed, cursing under her breath, and it was at that moment I realized she was crying. "Izzy, what's wrong?"

She whimpered. "She's gone again."

"Again? What happened?" I stood from the couch, rubbing a hand over my forehead.

"We got into a fight. Remember when I caught her sneaking out of the house last fall?"

"Yeah..."

"Well, she's done really well all this time. I haven't had any issues out of her for a while, but within the last month or so, I've caught her on the phone really late at night. Her grades have been slipping... I'm worried she's hanging around with some idiot guy again who's going to get her into trouble."

"Well, who was it last time? Have you talked to him? Or his parents?"

"We never found out," she said. "She swore she wouldn't see him again if we dropped it and, well, we didn't really have any choice in the matter."

"And now she's gone again? What about her cell phone? Can you check the records?"

"Darren's on the phone with our carrier now. We're locked out of our account, and he can't remember the password—"

I heard my brother-in-law say something in the background, cutting her off.

Eventually, she went on, "I just thought she might've come there. She had so much fun with you last summer, and she's always begging to come visit again."

"Well, she's not here, but I'll keep an eye out and let you know if I hear from her. Have you contacted the police yet?"

"We did, but, well, I don't think they're taking us seriously anymore. She's nearly eighteen, and this isn't the first time we've had to call them about her disappearing only for her to turn up in a day or so."

"Even so, they need to be taking it seriously."

"This isn't Cason Glen, baby brother. The cops here have more important things to worry about than girls who run away from home."

She was crying once more. I heard her sniffle, then blow her nose. Darren said something in the background again.

"Even in the city, it's their job to find her. Surely they're able to do something. Could you try one of those locator apps?"

"We'd downloaded one at one point, but apparently she's deleted it. I just don't know what else to do. We've told her how much we worry when she's gone, but it doesn't seem to get through to her. Nothing does. I can't keep living like this.

We can't keep sending out search parties just for her to show back up like nothing happened. What's going to happen the one time she's really in trouble and no one comes around to help?"

"Hey, that's not going to happen," I told her firmly. "She's going to be fine, and you know I'll help a hundred times if that's what it takes."

"Thanks." She sniffled again. "I just can't believe she ran off again."

"Do you want me to come there? I can help you look around, maybe we can talk to all of her friends…"

"No, it's okay. I'd rather you stay there just in case she does show up."

"Okay. If you're sure…"

"I am. But you'll call me if you hear from her, right?"

"The second I do, you know that. And same for you. If you hear anything, let me know."

"I will," she said softly. There was another noise from Darren, and she added, "Okay, I've gotta go. Talk to you soon."

"Okay, love you—"

The call ended, and I stared around my quiet house. My niece had never been a problematic child until recently, and she seemed to be on a quest to drive her parents past their breaking point. I'd tried to help out as much as possible, but hours away, I generally felt helpless. I glanced out the window, toward Stephanie's house and around the subdivision.

Would she come to me?

Would she come home at all?

Was she really in trouble this time?

Where are you, Soph?

CHAPTER TWELVE

STEPHANIE

I'd just lain down in bed for the night when there was a knock on my door. I sat up, adjusting the covers slightly. "Yeah?"

The door opened and Dominic stepped inside. "Mom?"

There was something vulnerable in his expression that cleared away all the anger and frustration I'd felt previously. It took me back to the nights he and his brother had come into our room after a storm, standing in the doorway, usually with one finger in their mouth—thumb for Raf, pointer for Dom—as they waited for permission to come into our bed.

I patted the corner of my comforter. "What is it? What's wrong?"

"Nothing," he said softly. "I'm sorry about earlier." At his words, I melted, the last bit of any bitterness washing away as he took a step toward me, sinking down on the end of the bed. "I don't know why I did it. I was just angry and…embarrassed. I didn't mean what I said."

"I know," I told him. "I know you didn't. I'm sorry, too, for embarrassing you. I know that you and your brother are growing up on me, but you've gotta help me out here. I'm just trying to keep you both out of trouble until you can graduate." I ruffled his hair. "You're good boys, I've always known that. And I know losing your dad has been tough on you…"

He nodded, his head hung down as he looked away. "Actually, that's why I was coming to talk to you."

I waited for him to go on.

"They're, uh, well, they're doing a memorial thing at school for Dad tomorrow. Principal Warner said we should ask you to come in for it."

"A memorial?" I asked, clutching my hand to my chest, tears suddenly lining my eyes. With the events of the afternoon, I'd nearly forgotten about the memorial for Ted. *But he might still be alive.* Memorials were for people who had died. I hated the way they were using that word.

"Yeah, for his birthday. They're gonna do a slideshow with pictures of him and a few of the students wrote poems or whatever… You don't have to come if you don't want to. It'll probably be stupid—"

"No," I cut him off. "No, I want to come. When is it again?"

"It starts at nine. They want us to say something about him."

"Something?"

"Yeah, just…anything, I guess. But I don't know if I want to."

"Well, I'm sure Principal Warner will understand that."

He nodded, then looked at me. "Will you, though?"

"Will I understand?"

"No. Will you say something? For all of us? So we don't have to?"

"Oh, I, uh…" I tried to think quickly. She'd said she wanted me to be there, but she'd never mentioned that I'd need to give a speech. I'd never been much of a public speaker and, without time to prepare myself, I was sure I'd make a mess of whatever pseudo-eulogy they wanted me to make, but, looking at my child's troubled expression, I refused to say any of that. Instead, I simply said, "Sure I can, sweetie. If that's what you want." I needed to pick out an outfit, wash my hair, call my boss... How had I nearly forgotten about all of this?

"I think he'd like that." He was quiet for a moment, then stood. "And it'll get Principal Warner off my back."

"I'm sure she thinks saying something about your father will help you and your brother feel better. Do you think you'd like to say something, even if it's just a few words? We could go up there together."

He waved me off. "Nah, you're better at that stuff anyway."

"That's not true. What does Raf think? He doesn't want to talk either?"

"No, we're both cool with you doing it," he said quickly. "Okay, I'm going to bed. I'll see you in the morning."

"Good night." It hurt me to watch him walk away. Hurt me to see him leaving me when we were connecting for the first time in months, if not years, but I had no choice. I couldn't be selfish with him. Had to take only what he was willing to give. Patience, I was learning, was the only way I'd ever connect with teenage boys. They'd come to me when they were ready, and I just had to be here.

He shut the door behind him and I covered back up.

Immediately, I began running through my checklist. I was supposed to have a shift for my day job as a 911 dispatcher, so I texted my supervisor, Mel, to ask if she'd have someone cover for an hour or two.

I'd worked with her for years, so I knew it wouldn't be an issue, but somewhere deep in my gut a part of me wanted her to say no. To tell me I needed to come in, just so

I could avoid what would most assuredly be an uncomfortable day.

Without waiting for her response, I laid my head on the pillow and closed my eyes, trying to think over what I'd say about Ted.

What are you supposed to say to honor someone who's missing when you aren't sad they're gone?

CHAPTER THIRTEEN

MICHELLE

J ude and I walked into the high school the next day just before nine o'clock. Many of the community members had decided at the last minute to host a memorial service for Stephanie's husband, Ted, on his birthday, and as he was the history teacher until the day of his disappearance, the school had agreed to host it.

As the town's sheriff, Jude's presence was all but required, and as the head of the school's PTA, they'd asked that I bring in baked goods and refreshments for a bit of mingling afterward.

Nothing like a memorial service to build up an appetite, right?

We set the stacked trays of cookies, fruit, and finger sandwiches down on the table next to the two liters of soda, pitchers of tea and juice, and red cups filled with ice.

Once I'd spaced everything out, making it look as neat as possible, Jude put a hand around my back and led us across the lobby.

On the wall next to the gymnasium, they'd added Ted's picture to a growing collection of photos. **In Loving Memory**, the letters above the group of frames read. There were more than twenty in total—teachers, faculty members, and students who'd died, even a few who'd gone missing like Ted had. It felt strange to see his photo up there, to know it was a sign that people were giving up on him.

Moving on.

The photos spanned decades, some in black and white dating back before we'd attended the school ourselves, but as much as I tried to scan the other faces, I found my eyes drawn back to our friend every time.

After a minute, Jude took a deep breath. "We should go in."

I nodded, trying to swallow down the lump in my throat as we made our way into the gymnasium. I looked for Caroline's face in the crowd of students all sitting in the bleachers.

There was music playing overhead—something soft and sweet. Elevator music, basically, keeping moods light as the students, teachers, parents, and other community members took their seats.

When I finally spied her, sitting between two girls I recognized from her class, I raised a hand over my head to wave.

She smiled back, her wave smaller than mine, and then returned to chatting with the girls.

I put my hand down, taking a seat next to Jude on the front row of the bleachers. He put his hand around my waist, holding me close as the music eventually died down and the principal made her way toward the lectern in the middle of the floor.

"Thank you, everyone, for coming. As you all know, we're here to celebrate, pray for, and preserve the memory of our beloved teacher, parent, husband, and friend. His students tell me Mr. Dupont is most remembered for having been fun and caring. He treated them like adults, rather than children. He valued their opinions and made each day feel like a new adventure. One particular memory I hear over and over when discussing Mr. Dupont, is the day he created a courtroom in his classroom and had the students each play a role in deliberating the case of the missing tests."

There was a chorus of sad, muted laughter throughout the room.

"And I know we all loved the way he'd go all out for the many school spirit, crazy hair and sock, and various theme days throughout the year." She paused, inhaling. "I, like many of the adults in this room, remember Ted Dupont as a teenager, sitting in these very same bleachers. He was always laughing. Always happy. Always the center of attention, the captain of the team, and the one you wanted on your side. He loved this school. He loved this community." She smiled sadly. "He loved every single one of you. There's no doubt about it. Mr. Dupont was a class act—pun intended, he would've loved that joke—and we were all very lucky to know him, for however long we had him."

There was another pause and she brushed her finger under one eye, dusting away a tear. "It feels strange to be doing this when we don't know that he's...gone. And"—her gaze fell to Stephanie in the front row, just a few spaces down from me—"of course, we hope he isn't. We hope he'll come back to his family, come back to us all... But, well, several members of the community and I thought today, a day we should be celebrating Ted anyway, a day most of us have celebrated Ted for…"

She blew air from her lips. "Well, I can't say how many years. Some of us are even older than him." The joke was met with another round of muted laughter. "Anyway, I thought today could help us all. I know we've all been in a sort of limbo state for a few months now, wondering and waiting, and it didn't feel right not to have something to honor him today. So, thank you all for being here. Thank you for helping me to support his family and his students, who all miss him more than is fathomable."

She offered a small smile. "And, now, I'm going to give the floor to his wife and sons, Stephanie, Dominic, and Rafael Dupont. So, everyone..." She started clapping, letting us know we should all be doing the same, so we did. The clapping started out quiet and uncertain—it felt odd to be cheering her on as Stephanie made her way to the center of the floor—but I quickly realized it was meant to be more of a means of support than an actual round of applause.

It was as if the sound propelled her forward, each step apprehensive, then reassured.

When she reached the lectern, she was alone. I glanced over my shoulder, wondering where the boys were. Why weren't they with her? She looked so alone, so frail standing there.

"H-hi—" The microphone squealed loudly, and when I looked back to her, she was adjusting it, a harsh wince on her face. "Hi, sorry. Um, as some, well, actually *all* of you know, I'm Stephanie, Dominic and Rafael's mom and Ted's—sorry, *Mr. Dupont's*—wife. I want to start out by thanking Principal Warner for doing this for Ted today. It really means so much to me and my boys, and I know he would be so *honored...*" She sniffled, stopping as she looked down with a finger pressed to the bottom of her nose and tried to regain her composure. When she looked back up, there were fresh tears glistening in her eyes. "He loves this school very much. He loves this community. And the boys and I have felt so wrapped in your arms, so loved and taken care of, since he disappeared. I can't tell you how much that has meant to us." She gripped the lectern tighter. "The boys asked me to speak for the entire family today, but I've always felt that we're all a family here, so those of you who are hurting like we are, those of you who are feeling heartbroken, like the pain will never go away, just know that it's not what he would've wanted. Wherever he is, if he's…gone, he would've wanted us to go on. To be okay." She looked to her right, where a blown-up photograph of Ted sat on a stand. "Maybe he'll come back to us someday, but if he doesn't, this community made him happy. You all made him happy. And, for that, his family will always be grateful. Thank you again for…all of this." She nodded, looking unsure for a moment, and then stepped back, walking away from the lectern without another word.

After a few painfully awkward seconds, Principal Warner stepped back up, smiling.

"Now, because this isn't a typical memorial and we aren't ready to give up hope on Mr. Dupont, I've also asked Sheriff Rivera to speak to you all today about the ongoing search and what we can all do to help." She started another round of applause, waiting for everyone to join in, which I happily did.

Beside me, Jude slipped his arm from my waist and stood up, walking toward the center of the room in his sheriff's uniform. His chest was puffed with pride, as it often was when dressed for work. He loved his job, loved being able to take care of our community, and in that moment, I felt my own chest swelling with a similar pride.

How had I gotten so lucky?

I'd gotten one of the good ones. So many weren't that lucky.

He shook Principal Warner's hand, an odd, cold gesture considering the memories we both had with Leilani going back to elementary school. But we weren't friends here, they weren't friends. Everything had to be kept professional, for the sake of the students and the community.

That's the strangest part of growing up in a small town, I guess. The fact that you already know so much about everyone you run into. Your doctor was in your algebra class, your mechanic took you to prom, your child's principal wiped your tears as you cried in the bathroom after a bad breakup, the manager of the restaurant where you have your Sunday dinners once made out with you under the bleachers of a home game.

There was so much history, and now that we were all adults, all upstanding members of society, our community, we had to pretend none of that ever happened. We had to be professional. Civil.

History, disagreements, old flames, and past rivals no longer mattered. Luckily, Jude and I had the performance down. Except for Jude's friendship with Ted and Enzo, it was as if no part of our past had ever happened.

Like we'd been born brand new the day we married each other. And, for all intents and purposes, we had. Our lives revolved around each other now, and it was a good thing, because marriages so intense, so honest, so loving... Well, I hated to even think it, but those were the marriages that wouldn't end with one of the spouses missing.

When he was in front of the microphone, he adjusted his belt and cleared his throat. "Thank you, Principal Warner. I'll keep this short, but I did want to say that we're all missing Ted, *sorry*, Mr. Dupont, and wishing he were here with us today. I know how you all must be feeling. Lost. Sad. Confused... Mr. Dupont and I were best friends growing up. We sat right where you're sitting many, many times. He was always silly, always fun," he paused, and though no one else could see it, I knew he was trying to prevent himself from crying, "always kind. I know it's already been said, but it's worth repeating: he loved it here. And we all loved him."

The room was filled with a still, uncomfortable silence as Jude collected himself.

"And, well, anyway, Principal Warner thought it would be nice if I gave a quick update on everything. So, as you all know, the investigation is still ongoing. If any of you have any information about Mr. Dupont's activities in the days before his disappearance, no matter how small—what you saw or heard or noticed could help us find him. If you think of anything, remember anything, absolutely any small piece of information could make a real difference. So, find me around town, call down at the station, or even let Principal Warner know." He smiled at her slyly. "She knows how to get ahold of me."

He looked at Stephanie then, though he'd been avoiding eye contact up until that point. "To the Dupont family, I just want to say, on behalf of the department, and, I think I can safely say, the community, our hearts are with you. Please let us know if we can do anything to help you through what I'm sure must be an impossible time."

Stephanie placed her hand on her chest and tilted her head down. And with that, Jude began to walk back toward me, replaced once again by Principal Warner.

He sank down next to me, kissing my head, and I rested my cheek on his shoulder for just a second, trying to comfort and be comforted by him all at once. The rest of the assembly went smoothly, several of the students stepping up to tell their favorite memory of their teacher or a reason why they missed him. Many students had written poems, one had painted a canvas she gifted to his family. By the end of the day, I don't think there was a single set of dry eyes in the gymnasium.

At one point, I looked over at a sign of movement and saw Enzo standing from his row a few seats back. He made his way toward Stephanie in the middle of a poem, while her shoulders shook with silent sobs, and I saw his arm slide around her shoulders. He was oblivious to my stares and the countless others.

Nothing existed except them.

How had I missed that?

I nudged Jude's arm with my elbow, using my gaze to point in the direction I wanted him to look. He did, turning his head slightly until he saw them, before immediately looking away.

He didn't meet my eye again, but I knew he finally believed what I'd told him. Something strange was going on between our neighbors, but what?

What exactly had brought them together if not the knowledge of our secret? Whatever Jude had done the night before last, he must've slipped up.

Now what were we going to do?

CHAPTER FOURTEEN

ENZO

After we left the school and made it back to the house, Michelle and I helped Stephanie carry the leftover food and refreshments into her house. I shouldn't have done it, but I wasn't heartless. After seeing her sob during the assembly, as much as I hated seeing her hurt and hated knowing that she was hurting because of him, I couldn't sit there and watch it happen.

I stood back as Michelle loaded up the refrigerator, trying not to feel awkward in the heavy silence. The pictures of Ted still hung on the walls in the living room, and I could see them from there, happy family photos that made my stomach rumble with jealousy.

"There you go," Michelle said. She slid the tray of fruit onto the top shelf of the mostly bare refrigerator before taking the sandwiches from me and placing them next to the pitcher of tea. "Hopefully that will give you guys a few easy meals."

"Thank you both," Stephanie said stiffly. I knew she didn't want me there, but she'd never say as much, not in front of

Michelle. Maybe I shouldn't have comforted her at the memorial, but what kind of jerk would I be if I hadn't? As angry and hurt as I was, she needed me at that moment. She had no one else, and I had to be there for her. Besides, no matter what she tried to accuse me of later, I hadn't done anything to make it obvious that we'd had anything but platonic feelings for each other.

"Of course," Michelle said. "Is there anything else we can do for you? I could help clean something or cook another meal or…run an errand, whatever you need."

"No thanks. I need to get ready for my shift anyway. I appreciate your help"—she met my eye finally—"both of you. Thanks for being there today."

"I wouldn't have been anywhere else," I said.

At the same time, Michelle said, "Of course."

We both hesitated. I was hoping she'd leave so I could talk to Stephanie alone, but Michelle wasn't budging. Perhaps she was planning to do the same thing, but why? What could she possibly have to talk to her about?

"Well, thanks again. I'll see you out," Stephanie said, gesturing toward the front door.

Groaning internally, I turned away, letting her lead us to the door and pull it open. If she would look at me again, I was going to try to let her know I wanted to stay and talk, but, seeming to sense it, she kept her focus on Michelle.

What else could she do?

She'd never acknowledged me in any real way in front of anyone, but particularly not the town gossip, who just happened to be married to the sheriff investigating her husband's disappearance.

Once she'd shut the door, Michelle and I nodded vaguely in each other's directions, waving goodbye, and then hopped into our cars and drove to our respective houses.

I stepped out, lost in thought about the events of the day when I approached the back door and froze.

I shut that when I left, right?

I would never have left without locking the back door, yet now it was cracked open slightly. I looked over my shoulder, considering hurrying across the subdivision to ask if Jude had come home yet, but I shoved the inclination from my mind. I didn't need the sheriff's help, even if he was my friend.

I could do this on my own.

I was sure it was nothing anyway.

I pushed the door open carefully, reaching for the bat I kept behind it, relieved to see it was still there, waiting.

I stepped forward, making my way through the kitchen slowly, listening for sounds that would tell me which direction to go.

The floorboard squeaked beneath my feet, and I froze. Suddenly, quick, careful footsteps could be heard on the second floor. My heart sped up as I tried to decide whether to rush toward or away from them. In the end, I didn't get a chance to decide, as I saw feet coming down the stairs. Black sneakers and jeans. Thin legs.

She came into view, a worried smile on her lips when she saw me. Her hand went to her chest as she huffed out a breath of relief.

"Jesus, you scared me, Uncle Enzo."

"Sophie, what are you doing here? How did you get in?"

"I still have the key you gave me last summer," she said, her brow furrowed. She tossed her long, blonde hair over her shoulder casually, moving forward with her arms outstretched for a hug. "I came to visit."

I scoffed, lowering the bat. "You came to visit? Haven't you ever heard of a phone?"

She dropped her hands at the chill in my tone. "Yes, I—"

"Sophie, do you have any idea how worried your mother is? She has no idea where you are. She's been calling you for days. She's scared out of her mind, calling the police, calling everyone in the family, and here you come walking in my door like it's a family reunion. You need to call her and tell her you're here so she can come and get you."

"I'm not going to do that," she said firmly.

"Like hell you aren't."

"If you make me, I'll just leave before she gets here. Wouldn't you rather me be here and safe than anywhere else?" She folded her arms across her chest, waiting for my answer.

"She's my sister, kid. This is probably kidnapping. Why are you here anyway? You know I won't lie to her for you."

"You don't have to lie. Just don't say anything for a few days while I crash here. I'll go home after that."

I laid the bat on the couch and scratched my temple, trying to think. "Why are you here anyway?"

"I just needed a place to chill out for a bit. Mom's been all over me lately, and I just had to get out of there, you know? Clear my head. Plus, I missed my uncle." She shoved my arm playfully. "Is that a crime?"

I ignored her question, not buying a second of it. "Look, I don't care if you stay here, but you have to at least tell your mom where you're at. She'll let you stay for a while. She just wants to know you're safe."

"She won't let me stay! She'll ground me for a month if I tell her where I am."

"Maybe she will, but maybe she won't. If you do the right thing, I can talk to her and try to convince her to give you a bit of time here, but I'm not letting you hide out or lying for you."

She murmured under her breath.

"What was that?"

"I thought you'd be cooler than this."

"Yeah, well, you thought wrong. Where's your car anyway?"

"I didn't drive," she said simply. It was the first time during the conversation she'd appeared less than confident.

"Well, we're three and a half hours from your house, so you didn't walk. How did you get here?"

"A friend picked me up."

My body tensed with a protective sort of anger. "What kind of friend?"

"Just forget it. I'll go home."

"You don't have to leave," I said, but she was already darting past me, an indignant look on her face. She reached the door before I shouted out, "Wait! Okay, fine!"

She froze, a small smile playing on her lips. "*Fine* what?"

"Fine. You can stay. For one night. Chill out. Clear your head or whatever you need, but tomorrow, one of us is calling your mom to let her know you're safe, do I make myself clear?" I wagged my finger at her, and she grinned as if it were precious rather than menacing.

"Yes." She bounced up onto her tiptoes. "Thanks, Uncle Enzo." She rushed forward, pressing her lips to my cheek and patting my chest. "You're the best."

She hurried past me and back upstairs, and I heard the guest bedroom door shut before the shower kicked on.

Stupid as she may believe me to be, I knew there had to be a reason she'd come to see me. I was a teenager once, too, albeit long ago, and I knew that mischievous look all too well. Whatever she was up to, I'd find out and, if it was anything nefarious, I'd be sure my sister knew the truth.

I was hard to lie to because I knew every trick in the book. I'd always been able to read people, to understand when they weren't being honest with me, and I knew Sophie was hiding something.

As I mulled over the thought, I glanced out the window, spying Stephanie's yellow Jeep as she pulled down her driveway. As she sped past, I couldn't help wondering which woman in my life had the most to hide.

CHAPTER FIFTEEN

STEPHANIE

I shouldn't have done it. I should've been stronger.

But I wasn't.

In the end, that's what it came down to. That's what it always came down to where Enzo was involved.

When Ted was still around, I'd never been strong enough to resist the pull of my old friend, my longest-held crush. Especially not when he lived just across the street while my husband, still living in our house, was busy breaking my heart and letting me down over and over again.

In school, Enzo hadn't looked twice at me. I was a nobody, but since marrying Ted, we'd gotten to know each other. He'd realized there was more to me than the nerdy girl he'd known in school. And, as we got closer, feelings began to develop. When Ted hurt me, Enzo had always been there to pick up the pieces, to comfort me, to tell me I was enough. That I was loved and beautiful and wanted.

It had been easy with him. No pressure. Nothing could ever be serious with us because I had Ted and he had Leslie.

Now that they were gone, the temptation was stronger and my excuses were weaker. There was nothing keeping us apart anymore, save for my own worry that someone seeing me in a relationship now would make me terrible. The town's judgments were heavy-handed and swift. Rumors caught on like wildfire in a desert. If someone believed I'd cheated on Ted, or even that I'd moved on too quickly, the town's anger with me would be unrelenting.

Everyone loved my husband. They revered him. He could do no wrong. I'd only been granted clemency because Ted had picked me. After years of being ignored, he'd started showing interest in me in high school, and then I was who he'd chosen to marry. If I was good enough for him, I was good enough for the town. But to betray that now—and any evidence that I was moving on would be seen as a betrayal, no doubt—would leave me with a shredded reputation. I'd get no second chance.

Enzo, ever popular, ever beloved, would never understand my predicament.

So, no, I couldn't move on, even for the sake of my own happiness. I had to do what was right for my sons.

They needed me, even if they didn't want me. They needed guidance, and I was the only parent left to give it. Nothing else mattered.

It was why I'd made it my mission to make better choices. Choices that didn't include sleeping with my neighbor.

But that night, after the memorial and a miserable shift at work, I'd made a choice. A terrible, stupid, insanely selfish one.

When I pulled into my driveway that night, spying a light on in Enzo's living room across the street, I sent him a text. An invitation.

The ball was in his court.

He could ignore me, call me selfish and tell me to leave him alone, or he could tell me he wanted me, too.

And, as I expected, within seconds, I had my response.

Twenty minutes later, he was at my door, his hair wet from a recent shower. There was a familiar, dark burning desire in his eyes when he pulled me to him.

"Where are the boys?" he asked, between passionate, hungry kisses in the hallway. He shoved me up against the wall, biting my bottom lip.

"Out for the night," I told him, allowing him to peel my clothes off as he led me through the living room, up the stairs, and toward the bedroom. He should've asked me if I was sure, and maybe I should've said something, but neither of us would.

We couldn't. We were powerless in each other's presence once we'd reached this point. Desire raged through me as we reached the top of the stairs, our lips never parting for more than a few seconds, and he scooped me up, his hands gripping my thighs as he carried me into the bedroom. Once inside, I flipped off the light and he placed me on the ground, running his hands through my hair as he nipped at my ears. I moaned, tilting my head back as my head began to grow fuzzy. He stopped, pushing me onto the bed with a low growl, and, in the silence, I heard him pulling his shirt over his head.

Within seconds, but still too long, he was back to me, his body on top of mine, the heat radiating from our skin combining. He ran his fingers down my body, tracing lines from my hip bone to my inner thigh, teasing and tempting, but never giving me what I wanted. Not yet.

I writhed underneath him. "Please, Enzo."

"Patience..." He pulled his hand away. "I've missed this." The heat of his breath warmed my neck, running his lips over my ear, then along my jawline.

Me too. The response was silent, drawing tears to my eyes. I squeezed them shut as I felt his kisses moving lower on my body, his tongue tracing a line toward my navel. My heart was pounding so hard in my chest I was sure the neighbors must be able to hear it. God, I missed him.

I let myself sink into the moment, thankful for the dark room that would conceal my tears as his mouth found the space between my legs finally. I couldn't think, couldn't move. It was familiar and warm, loving but intense. Passionate. Feverish. He still wanted me. Couldn't get enough of me. That hadn't changed. And, despite what I'd hoped, I hadn't stopped wanting him either.

In fact, why had I ever wanted to?

Why wouldn't I want more of this?

My toes curled with pleasure, my fists closing in his hair, and I forced the thoughts away, allowing myself to enjoy it.

As if it were the last time.

Who knew? Maybe it would be.

WHEN WE WERE FINISHED, we lay together, our chests rising and falling with heavy breaths under my comforter. We hadn't forgotten how to be together, or how good we were together, no matter how hard I'd tried to convince myself we would. I thought the time apart, the space, would make me realize it was never as good as I'd made it out to be with him, but I'd been wrong. Every inch of my body pulsed with a heartbeat as real as the one in my chest. It was as if I'd been stunned, my limbs weak and tingling.

How was it possible for anyone to make me feel this way?

How did he know just the right things to say and do? It was as if he'd gotten a lesson the rest of the world missed out on. Warmth spread throughout my body as I thought back over the previous hour, already hoping we'd go for round two.

"I missed you," he whispered, his chin resting beside my

temple, his warm breath in my hair. "I was starting to think I'd never...we'd never..." He trailed off. "I'm glad you reached out."

"I didn't want to," I admitted. "But I needed you. I needed this." I sighed. "I know I'm not being fair to you."

"Hey, we don't have to do that right now."

"Do what?"

"Anything but this," he said, trailing a finger across my jawbone, then down my neck and across my breasts. "I just want to be with you right now. I don't want to think about tomorrow or even an hour from now."

I nodded, breathing in his scent—leather and sex.

I heard the doorbell ring and shot up, my blood running cold.

"Are you expecting someone?" he asked. I flipped on the light and looked around the room, dismay setting in as I realized my clothes were all flung out across the house and on the stairs. I pulled open a drawer and grabbed clean pajamas, dressing quickly. "Steph, are you expecting someone?" he asked again.

"No, sorry. No." I barely spit the words out, so lost in thought I couldn't bring myself to speak. Who could've come over so late? Who would be at my house without warning? I checked my phone on the nightstand, but there was no missed call, no unanswered texts.

I rushed out of the room and down the stairs, scooping up clothes as I went. I made it through the living room, tossing the clothes into a pile on the couch, and rounded the corner so I could see the glass panels on either side of the front door.

What the hell?

I saw the police cruiser at the end of the drive and my heart rate sped up. *The boys. No.*

I moved forward quickly, grabbing hold of the door

handle and swung the door open. "Jude? Raf? Oh my god. What's…what's going on?"

Rafael stood in front of Jude, both facing me. My son appeared ashen, his expression unreadable.

Finally, after realizing Rafael wasn't going to answer, Jude spoke up. "I pulled him over down by Shadowen's Pointe with Tiffany Clarke. He was driving drunk, Steph. Swerving all over the road. Someone called and reported him. You're lucky it was me who found him and not Rodriguez. Henry wouldn't have let him off."

My hands began to tremble as I stared at my son, white-hot fury seething in my stomach. This had to be a joke. "You were *what?*"

Rafael stepped over the threshold and Jude went on, "I'm doing this as a courtesy for you, because I know what you're dealing with. What you both are. But if I catch him again, I'll have to arrest him. I took the Clarke girl home with the same warning."

"Of course. Thank you, Jude. I…God, thank you. It won't happen again. I'll handle this." I gripped my son's arm as Jude narrowed his gaze at him.

"I certainly hope so." He looked up, staring at something over my shoulder just as I heard the squeak of the floorboard behind me. I'd all but forgotten about my guest.

When I turned around in absolute horror, Enzo was in the middle of the living room, shirtless, his jaw agape.

"What's going on?" he asked.

"What the hell, Mom? What's he doing here?" Rafael demanded.

"I—" I had no excuse, no believable explanation for why our neighbor was in our house at such a late hour. Nothing but the truth, though I didn't need to spell it out for them. "Raf, I can explain." I couldn't. I didn't even know where to begin.

Jude was laser focused on Enzo, his jaw tight. I knew what he must think of me. His best friend hadn't been gone six months yet and already I'd filled his place in our bed. And with the third member of their trio to top it off. Even if, by some miracle, he didn't mention this to his wife, who would immediately rev up the town's rumor mill, I knew he must hate me. Why wouldn't he?

Enzo and Rafael watched me as I tried to figure out how I was going to explain the situation to Jude, to Rafael, to everyone. Before I'd come up with an answer, Rafael grabbed his stomach, leaning forward and launching the contents of his stomach onto the floor. The strong scent of alcohol and vomit permeated the air, salt in my already open wound.

How had I gotten here?

How would I fix this?

CHAPTER SIXTEEN

MICHELLE

I was in my office working late when I heard the front door open and shut, followed by the sound of Jude's heavy footsteps carrying across the floor. I checked the time, shocked to see it was already early morning, then exited the browser. Before I left the office, I grabbed a sticky note and jotted down a note to myself about where I'd left off, then stood from my desk.

I found him in the kitchen, a bottle of soda already in his hand.

"Rough night?" I asked, pulling down a wine glass from the cabinet and filling it halfway. I wanted to offer him one, to relieve some of the stress I saw on his face, but my husband wasn't a drinker. He rarely allowed himself a glass of wine and couldn't stand the taste of beer. Besides that, with such a small police force in our tiny county, there were too many instances where he was called in on a day off and he never wanted to have to refuse because he'd been drinking. So, more wine for me.

"Um, yeah... You could say that." He was staring into

space, not meeting my eyes. Suddenly, I began to feel worried. Panic quickly set in.

"What is it? What happened?"

"Um, well, I think you were right about Enzo and Stephanie."

I set my glass down. "They know?"

"No," he said quickly, looking my way at once. "Sorry, er, I don't think they know, but there's definitely more going on between them than we realized."

"What do you mean?" I cocked my head to the side, thinking back to the way he'd held her so closely during the assembly. When I'd gone back to her house and dropped off the food afterward, though, I tried to watch for any weird vibes or suspicious glances, but, if they'd existed, I'd completely missed them.

"Remember when you asked me if I thought losing their spouses had brought them closer together?"

"Yeah."

"I don't know how it happened, but you may have been right. I'm pretty sure they *are* together."

My brows drew down instantly. I couldn't lie and say I hadn't considered the possibility once or twice, particularly lately with the odd house visits and the way they'd acted at the assembly, but Enzo and Stephanie couldn't be more opposite. The idea that they could be dating, not hiding a terrible secret or plotting to reveal ours, was both perplexing and a great weight off my shoulders at once. "*Together* together? Are you sure? Enzo hasn't been with anyone since Leslie died."

"Until tonight, maybe."

"How do you know? What happened?" Why was he making me ask? Dramatic effect? "Tell me."

"Well, I picked up Rafael Dupont tonight, driving while

intoxicated. When I brought him home, Stephanie was home alone with Enzo."

"He could've just come to drop somethin—"

"They weren't dressed. She had her shirt on backward and he wasn't wearing a shirt at all." He let what he'd said sit with me for a moment before adding, "I'm telling you, the look on their faces… It was obvious they'd been caught red-handed. They're seeing each other. Who knows for how long."

I thought back to the day before yesterday, when I'd seen her outside sneaking around. "It would explain why I saw her running over to his house that day. And why she acted so suspiciously, if they're wanting to keep it quiet."

"Well, I could certainly see why they'd want to. If they've been having an affair, it all looks a little suspicious, don't you think? With Leslie dead and Ted gone."

I thought about what he was saying, toying with the idea in my mind as the truth of it weighed on me. "You're right. If they've been seeing each other longer than Leslie's been dead… You don't think they could've…" I trailed off, my fingers on my bottom lip. It wasn't possible, was it? They were our friends. No matter their secrets or scandals, I couldn't believe they'd be involved in anything so heinous.

"I don't know."

Suddenly, a strange thought crossed my mind. "Do you think Ted knew?"

He stared at me, and I wondered if he'd thought about that yet. Eventually, he shook his head. "I really don't know. If he did, he never mentioned it to me."

"I don't see how he could've been around Enzo so much if he knew."

"I don't see how Enzo could've been around him," Jude said.

"I can't believe they could manage to keep this a secret for so long. Maybe it *is* new."

"Maybe it is," he said. "But I'll tell you one thing, I think I was the last person they wanted to stop in tonight and find out what they've got going on." He chuckled to himself. "Well, maybe besides a drunk Rafael."

I couldn't bring myself to laugh at the joke as a sickly feeling filled my stomach. "And now you know."

"And now I know," he repeated, looking solemn.

"What are you going to do about it?"

He was silent, his lips pressed together as he stared at the floor, deep in thought. "I don't know."

"Enzo was cleared of Leslie's death, right? It couldn't have been him."

"Yeah, he had an alibi and none of his guns matched the bullet."

I winced at the words, still hating to think of what had happened to my friend. Our friend. Something as terrible as a break-in in Cason Glen was rare, but a break-in that led to a murder right in our subdivision had shaken us to the core. Everyone in Southwest Acres had gotten security systems within the days after, and I still flinched when I heard a noise in the house.

"But," Jude went on, drawing me back to the present.

"But what?"

"Well, we never considered Stephanie."

A lump formed in my throat and I tried to swallow it down. "She wouldn't…"

"I'm not sure I can sit on this knowledge, Michelle. If anyone were to find out I knew, I—"

My phone chimed in my pocket, cutting him off, and his eyes widened. "Is that her?"

I pulled it out, staring at the screen. "No. It's the group

chat for the neighborhood." I opened the message, my heart pounding as I read through it quickly. Jude moved to my side to read as well. "Mary and Darcy want to move the annual social from next month to...*this weekend?*" I kept reading.

"Darcy's parents are planning a visit unexpectedly, and they want to let them be a part of it."

Before I could even process the change in schedule, other replies had begun coming in.

Libby Dessen said, **Of course. No problem with us!**

Henry Otte said, **Sounds good. We'll be there!**

Evelyn Arnold said, **I can't wait to see everyone. Come hungry, I'll make my famous potato salad. If anyone knows of any single men...feel free to bring them. Wink wink. Only kidding! Ha ha.**

Isaiah Williams said, **K.**

I texted back too, joining in the chorus of excitement. **Can't wait! See everyone Saturday.**

With that, I switched my phone to silent and slid it back into my pocket, ignoring the buzzing. "We can watch them this weekend. See if we get a better feel for their relationship."

"Well, they're hardly going to let everyone know about it if they've been keeping it a secret all this time," Jude argued.

"Maybe, but now that you know, I wouldn't be surprised if they don't use it as an opportunity to cover their tracks and say it's all brand new."

He stared at me.

"It's what I would do," I said with a shrug. "We'll keep an eye on them this weekend and then you can decide what you want to do."

"Fine," he said. "But we have to be careful. If they're together, collective knowledge and all, you could've been right about everything... Maybe, I mean, I hate to say it, but we can't rule out the possibility that they know what we did."

"Well, if they do, now we have a secret of theirs, too." I tried to seem braver than I felt. Everything was going to be okay, wasn't it? It had to be. "And, if they killed Leslie in order to be together, theirs is worse."

CHAPTER SEVENTEEN

ENZO

"It's not the end of the world, okay?" Once the vomit had been cleaned up, Rafael had been sent to bed, and we were fully dressed, I tried to make Stephanie see reason. "It could've easily been a one-night thing. We're two consenting adults. What's Jude going to do about it?"

"Maybe nothing," she said, "but with just a little suspicion cast on us, our lives could change. This is a big deal, Enzo. I don't get why you don't understand that."

"I understand what you're saying, and I get why you're mad, but I didn't know what was going on. I couldn't just let you answer the door alone in the middle of the night. Not after what happened to—" I cut off, looking away, but I didn't miss the way her shoulders relaxed, the tension all but gone.

"Oh, God. Of course." She reached out a hand, placing it on my arm. "I'm so sorry. I didn't even think…"

"It just brought back all that fear, all the worry and guilt. If something happened to you, if I lost you like I lost her, I'd never forgive myself. You said the boys were out, and I couldn't see anything from the bedroom window except for the empty street. I just heard you freaking out and a man's voice, and I acted without thinking."

Her eyes softened, her fingers squeezing my arm lovingly. "It's okay. I understand now. Honestly, it's...well, it's not fine, but we'll figure it out."

"Rafael already knows now—"

"If he even remembers," she said with a dry laugh.

"I don't think it's something he'll easily forget." I laughed too, thinking of the mess he'd made and the way he'd cried as we cleaned it up, apologizing over and over.

"You're probably right about that. God, what am I going to do with these kids? They're trying to kill me, I swear." She leaned her head back, sighing.

"Well, maybe now's the time to let me help you."

Her body tensed again, and she lifted her head. "What?"

"Now that Rafael knows, it's not like we have a chance of keeping it from Dominic. And, once they know, everyone in town will know. So, why don't we use this as an opportunity to just come out with it and let everyone know all at once."

I expected her to argue, but to my surprise, she seemed to be mulling it over. "Maybe you're right. We could get ahead of the narrative and say that it's all very recent. That you've been helping me to deal with my grief, since you've gone through something similar, and we just...fell for each other."

I breathed heavily, leaning toward her. I lifted my hand to her cheek and brushed my thumb across her cheekbone as I stared into her eyes. "That part wouldn't be a lie, at least."

"No?" She batted her eyelashes at me.

"No." I pressed my lips to hers, my chest ready to explode with joy over the possibility of telling everyone the truth after all this time.

Well, part of the truth anyway. The only truth that mattered. We were in love, we were together, and nothing would ever again stand between us.

Our phones buzzed from the nightstand at the same time, and we froze, pulled apart, and reached for them.

A group chat we shared with everyone in Southwest and Northwest Acres. Typically, we only used it when someone's pet was missing or someone was hosting an event. I read over the message and then glanced at Stephanie, who was already staring at me.

"Looks like we have the perfect opportunity to tell everyone at once," she said. And, to my surprise, she was smiling.

Finally.

CHAPTER EIGHTEEN

STEPHANIE

I was a ball of nerves by the time the neighborhood social came around on Saturday. The social was an annual thing, something started by the first family to settle into our subdivision and my direct neighbors, Isaiah and Jen. They'd started out with just the families of Southwest Acres, but as time went on, we'd extended an invitation to our neighbors just down the road in Northwest.

Of all the events we hosted during the year, the social was by far the most popular and well-attended. If ever there was a perfect time for us to make our announcement, this was it.

I'd gone to every one in the past with Ted by my side, our boys in tow, but this time was completely different, and not just because I'd have a new date.

This year, I also wouldn't be attending with both boys accompanying me. As much as it pained me to make him miss it, I needed my son to learn his lesson. With that in mind, Rafael was grounded and not allowed to leave his room for the day. Dominic also, with no desire to show up to a party with his mother, had already left the house to join the neighborhood kids.

Enzo was supposed to pick me up at the door once the social was in full swing, a gesture that was sure to get the neighborhood gossiping enough to get the news out quickly. Honestly, I just wanted it to be over with.

When I heard the knock on the door, I stood, smoothing down my olive green and yellow sundress and checking my appearance in the mirror one last time. My heart was pounding so hard, sweat gathering at my hairline, that I was worried for a second I might pass out before I made it to the door.

Luckily I didn't, but when I opened the door, I felt even more breathless. *It should be illegal to look so good.* Enzo was dressed in fitted black pants and a light blue shirt, the sleeves rolled up halfway. His curly black hair had been styled, his chin boasting the five o'clock shadow I'd always loved. His gaze raked boldly over my body, beaming approval, and I couldn't help but do the same.

"You look beautiful."

"You…" I could hardly speak, so enamored by his devilish good looks. How long had it been since I'd seen him so dressed up? And now, I realized with glee, after today, I'd be allowed to appreciate his appearance as often as I wanted. Suddenly, everything I'd wanted from the beginning of our relationship was being handed to me. Could this really all work out? It was all happening, wasn't it? After all, what could go wrong? "You do too."

He looked down with a humble laugh before holding out his hand for me to take. I did, stepping out onto the porch. I shut the door behind me, not bothering to lock it.

Happy music blared through the neighborhood from the setup at Isaiah's house and the streets were filled with my mingling neighbors. As Enzo and I made our way through the crowd, I felt the eyes on us. Felt the stares. The questions. The whispers.

A flicker of apprehension coursed through me. Were we doing the right thing? Would this be a terrible mistake?

He squeezed my hand tighter, as if sensing my worry, and I forced a breath through my lips.

"Just keep moving," he said, his voice low.

"Oh my god! What is this?" came a loud question in the crowd. Evelyn Arnold rushed forward, her red hair pinned atop her head, red lips parted into a shocked 'O' shape. "How did I not know about this?" She slapped Enzo's chest playfully, winking at him. "You've been holding out on me, Mr. Mayor."

"Evelyn, good to see you," he said, dropping my hand for just a second as he hugged our neighbor. When he pulled away, he reached for my hand again, and I felt heat rise to my neck. The move didn't go unnoticed, and Evelyn looked positively delighted.

"It's about time you got back out there, honey," she said, looking only at him. "How long has this been going on?"

"Just a few weeks," Enzo told her, an answer we'd agreed on the night before. "Stephanie was really there for me after Leslie..." Evelyn nodded with a wrinkled expression of understanding. "And I returned the favor for her after Ted disappeared." He looked at me, a strained smile on his face. "It wasn't something we planned. It just sort of..."

Our eyes locked, and at the same time we said, "Happened."

"Oh! I love it!" She squealed with delight. "Well, I'm just so happy for you both I could scream." She glanced between us, but kept her focus mainly on Enzo. "You deserve to be happy. I was reading a book the other day about dating when you're our age. Making relationships work when you're already stuck in your ways." She chuckled. "I'll lend it to you, okay? It's really helped me. Lord knows the last guy I picked out was a total flop. Did I tell you he had a kid?" She pretended to gag. "Didn't even tell me about it until we'd been dating for three weeks. Can you imagine?" When she smiled this time, there was a smudge of her red lipstick on her teeth.

"I can't imagine. Anyway, thanks, Evelyn," he said, cutting the conversation short. If he didn't, we'd never manage to get away from her. I was grateful to leave, unable to help feeling uneasy at the hungry way she was staring at him. "It was great to see you."

With that, he pulled us away from her, toward the table of refreshments and the unpleasant-looking woman standing next to them. Libby Dessen watched us scrutinizingly as we surveyed the food. Her husband was busy filling glasses with juice for the kids.

"Did you bring something?" she asked, once we'd made it past her.

"Yes," Enzo said, stopping and turning around to face her. "I brought over the brownies this morning." He gestured toward the Tupperware container at the end of the table.

"I know that," she said. "I meant *her*." She said the word as if it were poisoned, hardly meeting my gaze. "Just because you're together doesn't get you both off the hook for bringing a dish." Enzo stared at her for a moment, and she feigned an apologetic smile. "I'm sorry, I don't make the rules. One dish per household. It's only fair."

"I brought the macaroni casserole," I said, gesturing toward the glass pan. "Dominic brought it down for me this morning."

"Oh," she said, her eyes widening. She tucked a piece of blonde hair behind her ear. "Of course. Great! Andy must've been out here when that happened." She cast an accusing glance at her husband who'd just struck up a conversation with another of the men from Northwest.

"No problem." I smiled stiffly and picked up a cookie

from the tray before Enzo pulled us away. We'd made it a few more feet when I spied Michelle and Jude making their way out of their house, their daughter Caroline just behind them.

They were perfect in every way. Caroline was quiet and studious, with her brown hair pinned back behind her ears and a simple white dress that hung extra loosely on her thin frame. Michelle—tall, gorgeous, and always so put together—wore a one-piece jumpsuit, black on bottom and bright white from her navel up, with a simple and elegant bow beneath her neck. She always managed to stand out, and with a tray of handcrafted hors d' oeuvres and her perfect husband by her side, there was no doubt she'd be the highlight of the spring social as much as she was the highlight of the fall festival and the summer bash.

The last thing I wanted was to talk to them—one of the perks of Ted's disappearance was that I no longer had to spend any unnecessary time with that woman—but I felt Enzo pulling us in that direction, and I knew I was powerless to stop it.

"Jude," he said, holding out his hand.

Jude took it, nodding at us both. "Hey, good to see you both together again."

"Yeah." Enzo laughed nervously. "You beat us to the chase with this announcement." He lifted our hands up, nodding his head toward them.

"Ah," Jude said, and I saw him exchange a glance with Michelle, who was studying me silently. Did she believe us? Or could she see right through the lie? "Yeah, I guess I did. Well, don't worry. I didn't tell anyone, so the secret's still yours to announce. *But*, judging by the stares, I'm guessing you already have." He laughed.

"Yeah," Enzo said, glancing behind us where I knew everyone must be watching. "We wanted to say thank you again about what you did for Rafael. We really appreciate—"

Jude put his hand to Enzo's chest, cutting him off. "Don't mention it. We're all friends, right? Neighbors. What good is that if we can't help each other out now and again?" He smiled, but it was reserved, almost cold. "Hey, listen, I've gotta talk to Henry really quick, but we'll catch up later, yeah?"

Before we could answer, he was jogging across the street with a hand in the air. Caroline walked away awkwardly and Michelle's gaze lingered for a second before she cleared her throat.

"I guess I should get these put down."

We nodded, watching her walk away as I felt the worry begin to surge in me again. They were acting odd, there was no doubt about it, but why?

They were normal on Wednesday at the school. Michelle had even helped me to bring home the food she'd made that day, so something had to have changed between then and now. Was it because of what had happened last night? Had Jude told her? Was she judging me? Was he? I knew them well enough to suspect that they were—that they were already starting to decide how to spin the scandalous story of my new relationship and our late-night visit. They'd be sure to tell everyone how I hadn't even waited until my husband returned to me. How I didn't care if he was alive or dead, I just had to find someone new—his best friend, no less. They'd make me the villain, destroy me in the eyes of everyone I knew.

"It's fine," Enzo said, obviously sensing my worry. "We have nothing to hide anymore and almost everyone seems really supportive. The ones who aren't will come around eventually and, in the meantime, we're going to have a lot of fun." His smile was convincing, but it did little to make me feel better. He began bobbing his head to the beat of the music Isaiah was playing, tugging on my hand to pull me out in the center of the grassy area where a few people were dancing.

As we moved, I scanned the crowd, looking for a familiar, friendly face. Who were we supposed to talk to at these things anymore? With Ted gone, everything felt out of place.

The neighborhood events had never been something I particularly enjoyed, but suffering through them was easier than being the only person in the community who didn't participate. Normally, Ted would have led us through, talking to parents and students, old friends and classmates, and I'd been happy to tag along. People were nice to me because I was with him. I was accepted by default. Invited out of obligation. It wasn't a great existence, but it was better than how things had been for me before Ted.

Now, it seemed the enchantment had worn off. The magical glow that came with being Ted Dupont's wife had faded. Now, people were avoiding me. Correction, they were avoiding *us*.

Enzo and me.

Because that's what we were now. An *us*.

Looking around the street at the judgmental stares of my neighbors, watching them whisper and mumble to each other, I began to feel dizzy. I pulled back as he attempted to twirl me.

"I can't—" I stepped off the grass, moving out onto the street.

It was too soon.

This was such a stupid idea. What had I been thinking?

Ted hadn't even been declared dead yet. My husband could still be alive.

He could still come back.

As I moved through the crowd, Enzo was next to me again, out of breath from dancing. "Are you okay?"

I had to calm down. I had to regain my composure. What

was worse than people seeing me moving on too quickly? People seeing me having a meltdown in the middle of our neighborhood.

I was horrified by the thought.

This was ridiculous. Ted wasn't coming back. I knew he wasn't. And, even if he did, would I want him after he'd abandoned us? What he'd done was unforgivable, but I'd be the one who needed forgiveness from the community if he did show up.

He abandoned me, but I'd moved on. It would be my moral failure they'd consider worse, I could already see it on their faces.

Scanning the crowd, I stopped suddenly as I landed on a familiar face.

"Hey…" I moved forward, trying to be sure I'd seen her right. "Do you see that girl over there?"

Enzo looked across the crowd, following my finger before his gaze landed on the girl. "Her?"

"Mhm. Do you know her?"

"Yeah, actually. That's my niece. Why do you ask?"

"Your niece is Tuesday?"

"Tuesday?" he asked with a confused scowl. "What are you talking about?"

"Isn't that her name?" I tried to think back. That was definitely what the boys had called her, wasn't it?

"No. Her name's Sophie. Why are you asking about her?"

"I…" I felt heat rush to my face. "No. Nothing. I'm sorry, I guess she just looks familiar. Hey, listen, I need to use the restroom. I'll be right back, okay?" I dropped his hand, and he nodded.

"Sure. I'm going to get us some drinks."

With that, we split up and I headed toward my house. When I reached the porch, I looked behind me, making sure

Enzo wasn't looking as I hurried back across the crowded street and toward the girl.

I didn't want to tell her uncle how I knew her or what I'd caught them doing. I'd been a teenage girl once—even if it felt like a lifetime ago—and I had no desire to get her into trouble, but I needed to talk to her.

She saw me coming and her jaw dropped, her eyes widening with recognition, but she didn't have enough time to escape. She took a step back and I saw that Dominic was standing next to her. When he saw me, he pulled his arm down from the shoulder of the girl on the other side of him, his face paling.

"Can I talk to you really quick?" I asked Sophie.

"Me?" she asked, touching her chest as if I could be talking to anyone else. "Why?"

"It'll just take a second. It's important."

"Mom, what are you doing?" Dominic asked, obviously chagrined.

"I should go," the girl said, taking another step back.

"Please don't. I want to talk to you about your uncle," I told her. She looked up, searching for him, then back to me begrudgingly before allowing me to lead her across the street. We stopped between Enzo's and Henry's houses, and I lowered my voice.

"What's going on?" she asked warily. "Did you tell Uncle Enzo about—"

"No," I cut her off. "No, I didn't. Not yet. But that's what I wanted to talk to you about. I'm going to have to tell him eventually."

"Why?" she whined.

"Because I'm an adult, and it's my responsibility to keep you safe. To keep my son safe."

"We were being safe. And honestly, it's, like, never going to happen again. Trust me."

"Okay, well, I'm not trying to pry, but you need to know that your uncle and I are dating. He asked me just a minute ago if I knew you, and I lied because I wanted to give you a chance to tell him the truth before I do. I won't lie to him again for you. Eventually, we're going to be introduced or he's going to bring you up, and at that point, I will have to tell him that we've met before. But I really think that should come from you."

"Why do I have to tell him anything?" she asked, her tone full of annoyance. "I mean, it's really none of your business. Or his, for that matter. I'm going home tomorrow. Uncle Enzo made me call my parents. I'm just in town for another day, so you don't have to worry about me."

"But you're dating my son, aren't you?"

She gave a dry laugh, though I wasn't privy to what was funny. "God, no. No offense. I mean, we were…" She shook her head. "No. We were just hanging out. It's over now."

"I hope it's not because of me," I told her honestly. "Because I don't have a problem with the two of you seeing each other. I just want you to be safe about it and, well, a little more discreet."

"No, it's not that. Sorry, he's just not really my type, and I don't think I'm his either, honestly. Seriously, it was just a one-time thing, and it'll *never* happen again."

"That's not how it looked to me. You two seemed pretty serious."

She looked down, kicking a rock with the toe of her sandal. "Well, I don't know what to tell you. Can I go?"

"So you aren't going to tell your uncle?"

"No, I'm not." She pursed her lips. "Do what you have to do, but it's already over, and like I said, I'll be gone tomorrow. Now, I'm going to go," she said firmly, no longer asking for permission.

"Okay," I said finally, watching her walk past me. When

she was a few steps away from me, headed back toward the crowd, I realized I still had one more question. "Hey!"

She glanced over her shoulder. "Yeah?"

"What's your name, by the way?"

She looked hesitant, and I wondered if she was going to answer at all, but eventually, she said, "Sophie."

"Sophie." I nodded slowly. "Do they call you Tuesday sometimes? Is it like…a nickname or something?"

She furrowed her brow. "No. Why?"

I shook my head. "No reason…" Suddenly, it felt as if a shard of ice slid through me, chilling my insides with a sickly wave of recognition. I knew why I'd been so bothered by the name, why I'd felt uneasy since I'd heard it. It was because I'd heard it used before. A nickname that took me back, filling me with disgust, regret, and then outright anger. It had been decades since I'd heard it, but it was there, tangled in the foggy, faded memory of my past. I tugged at it, as if tearing the recollection from the far recesses of my mind.

Yes. That was it.

I knew Tuesday because I used to be her.

CHAPTER NINETEEN

MICHELLE

I was standing next to Henry's house with Jude when I saw Stephanie leading a young girl I didn't recognize, though she was about Caroline's age, toward Enzo's house. Instinctually, I followed them, pretending to be cleaning up a patch of weeds in Henry's garden as I tried to listen to their conversation.

I didn't understand most of it, something about a Tuesday and an uncle, but I did manage to catch a few things about the girl dating Dominic Dupont. It wasn't as if that were rare news, the Dupont brothers were always dating someone new. I'd seen him dropping Henry's daughter off from a date just last week and he'd taken Jen's daughter out a few nights after that, so why hadn't I seen this girl around? I knew almost everyone in Cason County, so, if she was from around here, I should've known her. And, if she wasn't, why was she here now? As a date? I'd seen Dominic making out with a girl from Northwest earlier, and Rafael was nowhere to be found. It just didn't add up.

I didn't have long to ponder, though. The conversation didn't last long, and once the girl had rushed away from

Stephanie, I went around the opposite side of the house, trying to keep my eye on her. Why was Stephanie talking to the girl in the first place? Had something happened between her and one of the Dupont boys? It wouldn't be surprising.

She moved through the crowd with ease, smiling at people as she passed. I kept an eye on her, hoping to see her strike up a conversation with someone to give me a hint as to whom she'd come with, but instead, she stopped at the refreshment table. Suddenly, I saw my opening. Without hesitation, I walked up next to her, smoothing out a napkin that had been knocked from its place in the stack and pouring myself a drink.

"Oh, hello there. I don't think we've met yet." I pretended I'd only just noticed her. "I'm Michelle Rivera, the sheriff's wife. I live there." I pointed toward our home. Though they were all beautifully designed homes, it was undeniable that ours was the most well-maintained and tastefully decorated. I felt pride every time I got to show it off. "Do you live in the neighborhood?" I knew she didn't.

"Oh, no. I'm visiting my uncle."

"Who's your uncle?" I rested my hip on the table, hoping to convey that this was just casual chitchat, rather than an inquisition.

"Enzo Barone."

My jaw dropped. "Wait a second, you're Isabel's daughter?"

She nodded. "You know my mom?"

"I sure do. She and I go way back, even cheered together in high school. Is she here with you today? I haven't seen her in years..." I scanned the crowd, hoping to see my old friend.

"No, she's not with me. I've been staying with my Uncle Enzo this week," she said. "Today's my last day here."

"You've been here for a week?" I raised a brow, shocked I hadn't seen her.

"Give or take a few days, yeah." The girl popped a cheese cube into her mouth, her gaze dancing across the various faces that moved past and around us.

"Well, that little sneak. He didn't mention he had company. How wonderful of you to visit him. It's really a shame your mom couldn't come. Maybe next time." She smiled, but didn't meet my eye and made no effort to say anything else, so I went on. "What's your name, by the way?"

"Sophie," she said, popping a blueberry into her mouth.

"Nice to meet you, Sophie. This is your first time coming to Cason Glen, isn't it? How are you liking your stay? It's really a beautiful community. Are you settling in okay? Anything I can do to make you feel more welcome?"

"Oh, no, it's fine. I've been here before."

"Yeah?"

"Yeah, I came last summer," she said.

"Really? I don't remember seeing you."

"I was here." There was a hint of annoyance in her tone, and I sensed the conversation would soon be cut short.

"Well, that's great. I guess we just missed each other. But you'll probably know my daughter, Caroline." I pointed across the crowd toward where Caroline stood with a few of the neighborhood teens, a separate group than Sophie had been in. "She's the tall one."

Sophie was quiet, studying her. Eventually, she said, "I've seen her around, yeah."

"Well, don't be a stranger. If you're ever here with your Uncle Enzo again, come by. Caroline would be happy to show you around the town."

"Oh, thanks." She twirled a piece of her hair, picking up another piece of cheese, then a handful of cherry tomatoes, and placing them onto a small plate.

"Have you made many friends here? I think I saw you talking to Dominic Dupont earlier."

"Oh, I, uh, no not really. I haven't had much time to make friends. I've pretty much just been hanging with Uncle Enzo."

"What about last summer? Surely you spent time with someone then."

She looked up at me, a strange sort of panic in her eyes. Suddenly, she set her plate down, dusting her hands. "I'm... I'm sorry, I need to go." With that, she scurried away from me, her plate of untouched food still sitting on the table.

Was it something I said?

CHAPTER TWENTY

ENZO

I was searching the crowd for Stephanie when I stopped in my tracks, cocking my head to the side. Why on earth was Michelle talking to Sophie?

As far as I knew, they'd never interacted before. Perhaps it was just friendly neighborhood small talk, but it didn't seem that way. Michelle was staring at her with a strange, pinched smile on her face.

Sophie, on the other hand, somehow looked even more uncomfortable. As I watched the interaction from afar, trying to understand what I was witnessing, I realized something was very wrong. I needed to intervene, to save Sophie from whatever gossip Michelle would be trying to pry out of her.

Izzy would never forgive me if I let Michelle Rivera get wind of the fact that her daughter was a runaway. Just as that realization set in, I started forward, but Sophie was putting down her plate, shaking her head, and walking away. She looked upset. What had happened?

I headed in her direction, trying to fight my way through the crowded grassy area.

"Sophie, hey! Sophie, wait!" I called, darting around a couple dancing as she passed in front of me, several feet away and oblivious to my shouting. "Sophie!" I called again, but she didn't stop. If anything, she seemed to be picking up speed. She continued to jog farther and farther away from me, then made a sharp left turn and headed toward my house.

I spun around, racing after her. "Sophie! Hey! Wait up!" She flinched at the sound of my voice, glancing over her shoulder at me, then rolling her eyes. As she reached the grass of my yard, she stopped finally, turning around with a dramatic drop of her shoulders.

"What is it?" she demanded.

"What's…wrong? Are you done hanging out?" I asked, still trying to catch my breath, my hand pressed to my chest.

"No. I just need to pee. Why are you chasing me?"

"I thought you might be upset."

"Why would you think that?" She scowled and, without waiting for me to answer, turned back around and approached the front door, disappearing inside quickly.

As the song that had been playing over Isaiah's speakers ended, everyone began to clap, as they often did after a song they particularly enjoyed, as if there were an actual band waiting for the applause.

I looked around, frustrated that I still hadn't found Stephanie. Dominic was nowhere to be found either. I spotted what appeared to be Evelyn reporting the broken board in her fence to Jude. Michelle was still alone, near the refreshments, as her eyes scanned the crowd. It was where you could find her at every social event, taking in everything happening throughout as she waited for a chance to pick up on some sort of scandal. It pleased her in a way I couldn't understand. It always had. Michelle traded in secrets, it was her currency, and I realized then, I needed to shop.

I approached her, noticing as I got closer that she appeared shaken up, a rare sight for the woman most in our town considered perfectly put together.

"You okay?"

She squeezed her eyes shut for a second, then opened them, as if coming out of a trance. "Sorry, what?"

"You okay? You look upset."

"Oh, no." She waved off my concern. "I'm fine. Just tired, I think."

"What were you talking to Sophie about?"

"Sophie?" Her brows rose with apparent confusion.

"My niece, Michelle. The girl you were just talking to."

"Hey," a sharp voice called, and I looked over, surprised to see Jude heading toward us. "Where've you been? I thought I'd catch up to you later, but everyone in town has managed to stop me for something. Had to make the rounds, you know." He smiled with one side of his mouth as he reached us.

"Yeah, that's how it usually goes. I was just asking Michelle what she was talking to my niece about."

Jude looked at Michelle as we waited for an answer and, as could be expected, she didn't miss a step. "I was just asking her how she was liking her visit to Cason Glen. I can't believe how much she looks like her mother. I didn't place it until she said who she was. How is your sister, by the way? I almost never hear from her anymore. She's not very active online, is she?"

"I'm not really online, so I wouldn't know. Was that all you talked about?" I asked.

"Well, I told her Caroline would love to show her around if she ever needed someone her age to hang out with, but that was the gist of it."

"That's a great idea," Jude said, then turned his attention back to me. "What's the problem?"

"There's no problem," I said, my eyes darting back and forth between them. "But Sophie seemed like she was upset about something. I saw her run off and go inside, but she wouldn't talk to me about what was wrong. And then, when I looked over here, you seemed upset, too. I thought maybe something had happened between the two of you."

"Was she upset?" Jude asked her. "Are *you* upset?"

"No, I'm not upset, sweetheart. And Sophie seemed fine when she left me. She just mentioned something about needing to go," she said, her tone light and easy. "It would be news to me if she was upset. It certainly wasn't because of anything that happened between us. Honestly, Enzo, what do you think I could've done to the girl?"

I shook my head, groaning internally. It was useless with Michelle. If she had said something to upset Sophie, she'd never admit to it. I wouldn't put it past her to accuse the girl of breaking into our event to steal a bit of food. When she knew you, Michelle was kind and helpful. But to outsiders, her icy personality knew no bounds. If she thought Sophie had crashed the party, I couldn't imagine what she would've said to her.

I stared at the plate of untouched food, backing away. "I don't know. It's probably nothing. Never mind. I'll talk to her. Have you seen Stephanie, by the way?"

"Last I saw, she was going into the house," she said simply. "After she talked to Sophie."

"Wait. You saw Stephanie talking to Sophie?" I began scanning the crowd again. When had that happened? And why? As far as I knew, she'd never even met my niece.

"Mhm, they were over by your house talking just before I spoke to her. Honestly, it's so nice to see everyone welcoming her, don't you think? I'm sure it's hard for her to come here…"

I stopped searching, diverting my attention back to

Michelle. "What do you mean by that? Why would it be hard?"

She appeared flustered. "Oh. Well, I mean, after Leslie, I just assumed... They were close, weren't they? Aunts and nieces usually are."

I felt my jaw tighten, a muscle above my eyebrow twitch. Why would she bring that up right now? Jude put a hand to her arm, as if trying to warn her away from the subject. It wasn't exactly casual brunch talk. "Yeah, I guess they were close."

"I assumed. How long is she going to be in town for? Like I told her, Caroline would love to have a new friend."

"She's leaving tomorrow," I said stiffly. "Anyway, I need to go find Steph."

"Oh, yes," she purred. "Can't let her out of your sight for too long." Her laugh was warm and smooth, like honey. "I remember those days."

Without a response, I turned away from her and began moving through the crowd again.

"Have you seen Dominic's mom?" I asked the group of teens I'd seen Sophie with earlier.

They shook their heads.

"No."

"Haven't seen her."

"I don't think so."

"I don't remember."

I put my hand up, waving a thank you, and headed in a different direction. "Have you seen Stephanie? Did she come back out of the house?" I called to Evelyn as I zipped past her.

"Haven't seen her," she called, continuing on her way.

I rushed up her long, concrete walkway and then up the porch stairs, rapping on her door. It had been nearly an hour since she'd left me at the party, and, as I looked through the crowd now, I realized Dominic was still gone too. Where was she?

After a few minutes, I knocked on the door again. There was no noise coming from inside the house, no sounds of footsteps or talking, running water, or a television. Rafael, at least, was supposed to be home. I stepped back, looking up at his window, but his blinds were closed, curtain in place.

I stepped forward once more, knocking again. This time, I shouted, "*Stephanie?* You in there?" I looked over my shoulder, relieved that no one seemed to notice the noise I was making thanks to the loud music. A small group doing the electric slide had begun to congregate in the grassy center of our cul-de-sac.

Just then, I heard footsteps coming down the stairs inside, and within seconds, the door swung open and Stephanie stood in front of me, tears in her eyes.

"I need to be alone," she said, trying to shut the door, but I stopped her.

Why did she need to be alone? Had she discovered my secret?

CHAPTER TWENTY-ONE

STEPHANIE

"What happened?" Enzo asked. He wanted me to let him in, both into my home and into my world, but I couldn't. I couldn't tell him anything.

I shook my head, drying my tears as quickly as they fell. "I'm sorry I bailed. It was just too hard. I need some space right now."

"Please wait. Tell me what's going on. What was too hard?"

"Everything," I said, as honest an answer as I could give.

"Talk to me. What can I do?"

"I just need time, Enzo. You didn't do anything wrong. I just need to be alone for a while. Please respect that."

"Okay, do you want me to find Dom? Tell him you went home? Or do you want me to have him come home?"

I glanced behind me into the house. "No, I don't want him here right now. He's with his friends. He'll be fine."

"Oh…okay. Are you sure everything's alright? There's nothing I can do to…help in some way?"

"There's nothing you can do," I told him, swiping another

tear away. I gripped onto the door tightly, trying to maintain my composure. "I need you to go."

"Wait!" His palm slammed into the door as I moved to shut it, startling me. "I'll go, fine. But I need to ask you something first."

I stared at him, waiting. "Then ask me."

"Were you talking to Sophie earlier?"

So he'd seen me. I should've been much more cautious, but I hadn't been thinking. I never thought things through enough. "I was, yeah."

"What about?"

"You should ask her."

"She's a teenager, Steph. She doesn't tell me anything." He cocked his head to the side gently, trying to connect with me, and if there was anything he could connect with me over in that moment, that was it.

I sighed, using both hands to wipe my eyes. "Do you want to come inside? I can't talk about it out here." I stepped back, but he hesitated.

"You're sure?"

"As I'm gonna be." I pulled the door open farther, allowing him inside. Looking relieved, he walked past me and I shut it behind him. Together, we walked into the living room and sat down on opposite ends of the tan, leather sofa. I turned to face him.

"I, um, I caught her and Dom together in the driveway four days ago."

"What do you mean you *caught them?*"

I raised my brows and he seemed to catch on. "They hadn't crossed the line, but they were close. I caught them and sent her home, but I had no idea who she was. If I'd known she was your niece—"

"Hang on…" He held a hand up, cutting me off. "Four days ago? She didn't get into town until Wednesday."

I thought back, counting my days. "No, it was definitely four days ago, Tuesday afternoon."

"Well, she didn't come to my house that night. Where did she go?"

I swallowed, suddenly feeling guilty for sending her away without making sure she made it somewhere safe. "I don't know. I offered to take her home, but she ran off. She was on her phone. Maybe she has another friend nearby?"

"Maybe," he said, staring off in thought.

"Anyway, she's with you now and safe, which is what matters, but when I saw her and realized who she was, I confronted her and told her she should tell you first, before I did. So, you should give her the chance to tell you before you say anything."

"I'm not going to say anything anyway," he said with a shrug.

"You aren't?"

"She's almost eighteen, Steph. We were all doing much worse by that age. What kind of hypocrite would I be to say anything about her doing the same?"

"Don't you think her parents will want to know? Not to... get her into trouble, but so they can talk to her about safety and consent and—"

"Maybe, but it won't come from me. I love her, don't get me wrong, but this conversation goes so far above my parenting responsibilities it's not even funny. Besides that, my sister's barely able to keep track of her now. If she runs off because of a fight over something like this, we may never see her again. I'd rather they just keep her happy until she's old enough to do what she wants. *Which* she basically already does anyway."

I couldn't believe what he was saying. Perhaps it was just the fact that I was a parent while he was not, but I was irritated by his cavalier response. We'd not run out of time to parent our children just because they were teenagers. We were still responsible for them, expected to prepare them for the real world. Sophie's parents deserved to know what she'd been up to.

"Don't you think her parents should have the choice of whether or not to discuss it with her?"

He studied me, obviously not missing the sharpness of my tone. "You're probably right," he conceded, but it didn't seem to be sincere. "It's my fault for trying to be the cool uncle. I'll tell Izzy when she comes to pick Sophie up."

"I don't want to shame her or get her into trouble, I just think once they hit this age, there are conversations that should be had. And you shouldn't take that opportunity away from your sister."

"I'm agreeing with you," he said, nodding. "You're right. I should've never questioned your judgment."

Tears began to fall from my eyes and I leaned forward over my knees, my face buried in my palms. "Well, someone should. I have no idea what I'm doing anymore, Enzo. I've messed everything up so badly."

He slid toward me, the leather of the sofa creaking under his weight, and I felt his arm go around me as he pulled me into him. "You're being too hard on yourself. Is this because you caught them together? Is that why you're crying? Because you feel like it means you failed? Seriously, I mean they're teenagers, Steph. It comes with the territory. You're an amazing mom, but nothing you could do would prevent your sons from turning into men."

"No, I—" I caught myself before I'd said too much. "It's not about catching them together, not really. It's…complicated."

"Complicated how? Can't you talk to me? You know you can trust me with anything. We've told everyone we're together now, the hard part's done. Let me help you through this."

"It's not that. I do trust you, but this isn't something you can help me through. It's just that, well, it's embarrassing and personal. No matter how much I trust you, I just don't know how to talk to you about this." I rubbed my eyes forcefully. "I'll be okay. I just need time to process everything."

"But if not me, then who will you talk to?"

"No one," I said firmly.

His palm caressed my shoulder. "You can't keep handling this all on your own. With Ted gone, so much has fallen on you. You need to let me help carry some of the weight. It's going to break you if you don't."

I felt fresh tears stinging my eyes and looked away. "I don't even know where to begin. It's stupid. I'm overreacting."

His finger grazed my cheek. "It's not stupid, and I promise I won't think you're overreacting. Talk to me. Let me be here for you. Please?"

I sniffled, standing from the couch. I couldn't look at him while I talked about it. It was too much.

"You and Ted were friends in school, right? I mean, I know you were, but how close were you? He never said how much he told you about…everything."

Behind me, I could hear him adjusting on the couch again. He cleared his throat. "Um, well, I wouldn't say we were *best* friends, not like him and Jude, but we played ball together and went to the same parties and hung around with the same crowd. It's not like there were a ton of kids to choose from as friends in Cason Glen, but I considered him a friend, yeah. I'm not sure what you mean by *everything*, though."

I turned back around, meeting his eyes as I framed the next question in my mind. I needed to see the truth of his next answer for myself. "Okay, so, when I say the phrase 'she was a Tuesday' or 'she's my Tuesday' does that mean anything to you?"

I watched his expression grow more confused as his eyes rolled toward the ceiling, his forehead wrinkling. "I don't think so," he said eventually. "Should it?" If he was lying, he was believable.

I shook my head, facing the mantel and running my finger across it, brushing the dust from its top. "It was something stupid that Ted used to do when we were all in school. He'd name girls after the day of the week he slept with them. Tuesdays, Wednesdays, Fridays, etc. He had a different girl for each day, some of us that he repeated more than others, but, even the ones he repeated, they'd only get him for that specific day." I tried to think, running my hand through my hair anxiously. "There was some stupid poem about it... Like the old rhyme, you know the one... Monday's child, Tuesday's child, and so on... I don't remember what it was, but he used to joke about it with me. Monday's girl is wild in bed... Tuesday's girl...gives great head, maybe? Wednesday's girl is a double D, Thursday's girl has only slept with me... I'm sure I'm getting this wrong, but it was something like that. I don't remember. Is any of this ringing a bell?"

When I looked back, his face was ashen, his voice breathless, "I always thought that was just a joke."

"So you did know about it?"

"I mean—" He ran his thumb over his palm, and I watched the white imprint form and fade. "I heard rumors about it. Some of the guys would talk about it as a joke or sing it in the halls. Locker room talk and all that, but I never knew anyone who actually *did* it. Ted was...well, he was Ted. You know how he was back then. He said stuff and we all went along with it and pretended it was cool, but we knew he wasn't serious. Ted was always popular, sure, but a different girl every day of the week? Even for him, that seemed far-fetched. He was just a kid. We were all just kids."

"Well, it wasn't a lie with Ted, and do you want to know how I know?" I grimaced. "Because I was a Tuesday girl, and like an idiot, I was proud of it at the time. I was proud that he'd found space for me in the lineup," I said bitterly.

"He was an asshole." He stood up and closed the space between us, cupping my face in his hands. "He was an asshole, and he was blind for not seeing what he had with you. You're not a Tuesday, Steph, you're an every day, for the rest of my life." He pressed his lips to mine, and I felt tears cascading down my cheeks, transferring to his skin. When we broke apart, he kept his face close to mine, our noses still touching. "I don't want you to think about him anymore. I don't want him to hurt you again."

"It's not—" I sniffled, swiping a finger across my cheek. "It's not that. I'm not crying over Ted or that stupid memory. It's just that, well, the other day, I heard the boys refer to Sophie as *Tuesday*, but, I mean, it's been more than two decades. I wasn't thinking about that poem or the nickname or any of it… I haven't thought about any of that in so long. I just assumed it was her name until you told me it wasn't."

His expression hardened, and I knew he finally understood at least some of the weight of what I was telling him. "You're saying Sophie was a Tuesday for Dominic?"

I nodded slowly. "I'm so sorry… I just, I knew they weren't perfect, but I never believed they could be so heartless. I know it probably seems like harmless locker room talk to you, but I remember feeling so helpless with Ted back then. I cared about him so much, and I knew I was just another girl to him, but I didn't care enough about myself to stop it. I wish I had. I've wished so many times that I could've gone back to that time and made him stop it. And, with the boys, I've tried so hard to raise them to be different from their father, and I thought I'd done it, but apparently not. Apparently they're going to be just like him. I've failed them so badly."

"That's not true," he said, his thumb stroking my cheek. "It's not. You haven't failed them. Your boys will be different, they'll be good boys, good men, because they have you." He kissed my nose, but it did little to bring me comfort because it simply wasn't true. I hadn't done enough to ensure they turned out nothing like him. "And anyway, he calmed down after we graduated. After you got married. The boys will, too."

"That's just it, Enzo, what if they don't? Ted didn't, not really. He hid it better, maybe, but he never changed."

"What are you saying? He...cheated on you?"

I gave a dry laugh through my tears. "That's putting it mildly."

"You never told me."

I nodded. "I know. I couldn't. It was too embarrassing."

"I don't understand. Why didn't you leave him? We spent all those years sneaking around, and you could've just been with me."

"I was trying to do the right thing for the boys. I was trying to play the role of happy mother. Ted always said his mother leaving when he was young damaged him so badly. I couldn't help always wondering what would happen if I did the same. I didn't want them turning out the way he did to be my fault—"

"That could never happen."

"But now he's run off with someone else and, what do you know, it's my fault anyway."

"Stephanie, that's not true."

"What am I going to do, Enzo? I can't control my husband. I can't control my sons. I can't control my life anymore. I'm failing at everything I've worked so hard to save and—"

"Hey," he said, wrapping me in his arms so my face was shoved into his chest. I released the sobs I'd been fighting back, allowing myself to fall apart, to let down the wall I'd so carefully constructed throughout the years. "This is not your fault. None of it." He rubbed my hair, his voice soothing in my ear as he tried to convince me everything would be okay.

Try as he might, it was no use.

Nothing would ever be okay as long as I held on to the final secret left in me.

And I would. I had no choice.

It was the final brick in the prison Ted had carefully constructed before he left me to die in it.

CHAPTER TWENTY-TWO

MICHELLE

As the day began to wind down, families started returning to their homes, breaking down tables, and dividing up the remaining refreshments. I made the rounds, waving goodbye to everyone and helping out where I could as I searched the crowd for my husband, but eventually returned to find Jude already waiting for me near our yard. He grinned, holding the empty tray of my homemade cranberry crostinis.

"You ready to go?" he asked, a happy-go-lucky grin on his face.

I nodded. "I was just looking for you. Have you seen Caroline?"

"I helped Ben Brockwell carry some of his stuff down to Northwest, and I got distracted by the den. They just redid it, an eighty-five inch TV." He held his hands out, showing the size. "We need one of those."

"We don't have the wall space," I told him lightly. "Or the money, for that matter."

"We'll knock down a wall. You don't really need the sitting room, do you?" He laughed, and I wrinkled my nose at him, rolling my eyes playfully. "Only teasing. Caroline was… I thought I saw her with her friends earlier, but it's been a while," he said, looking around, his brows drawn down as he searched. He pulled out his phone, dialing her number just as his eyes widened. "Ah, there she is!" He pointed straight ahead over my shoulder, and I spun around to see Caroline helping Evelyn carry in a few half-empty pitchers of tea and lemonade.

"Care!" he called, trying to get her attention. She looked up at the sound of her nickname. "We're going home. Come on as soon as you're done with Evelyn."

She nodded, climbing the porch steps, and Jude and I spun around, making our way across the street and back home. Jude carried the empty tray in one hand and used the other to lace his fingers through mine.

He smiled at me with a longing gaze that I recognized. He was happy. These events were a highlight for us. We'd always found it fascinating to get to see our neighbors and friends in such a relaxing, warm environment. The cul-de-sac was mostly empty as we reached our porch, the sun beginning to set.

"Good night, all," Isaiah called, his loud voice echoing through the silence just before I heard the roar of his garage door closing.

"Good night," Jude said loudly, echoed by Henry and then Jenn.

Once we were inside, I brought the dish to the sink and Jude headed for the stairs. I began to fill the sink with water, staring mindlessly out the window into the backyard.

It was only minutes until I heard the front door open again and Caroline's careful footsteps heading down the hall.

"Caroline, could you come help me for a moment?"

"Sure, what with?" She appeared in the room behind me, and I watched her reflection in the glass pane.

"Just a few dishes, please." I pulled open the drawer and held out a clean dish towel. "There's not enough to run a full load in the dishwasher, so I thought we'd just go ahead and knock these out before bed."

She stepped forward, taking the towel and placing her hand over her mouth to stifle a yawn as I began to scrub the first dish.

"So, did you have fun today?"

"Yeah, I guess so."

"Who did you hang out with? I looked for you a few times with Taylor and Allison, but I didn't see you with them as much this year."

"Yeah…" She trailed off. "I didn't really hang out with them. Henry was trying and failing to teach me to play corn hole for a while, and then I helped Evelyn keep the drinks refilled."

"That sounds fun. I'm sure your friends missed you."

"I doubt it. We don't really hang out anymore…" For a second, I thought she was going to say something else, her mouth open after a breath, but after a minute, she closed it without a word.

I nodded, understanding we needed to change the subject. She'd lost friends after everything happened, distanced herself after going through what she had, and I didn't want to hurt her by bringing it up anymore. "Well, it was gorgeous out, wasn't it? The weather really helped us out this year."

"Yeah, at least there was no rain again." She took the dish from me and began drying slowly before moving to the bottom cabinet beside the fridge to put it away.

"Hey, I wanted to ask you something."

She sifted through the cabinet, making room, and called over her shoulder. "Yeah?"

"Do either of the Dupont boys have a girlfriend that you know of?"

She shot up at the question, her body rigid. "Why would you ask me that?"

"I was just curious. Most of the other teens in the neighborhood seem to be starting to date, but I can never pin down who the boys are dating."

She raised a brow dubiously. "Well, it depends on which day you're asking, I guess."

"What do you mean?"

"Nothing, it's not important." She closed the cabinet and walked back toward me, taking the next dish from my outstretched hand.

"No, tell me what you meant," I coaxed her. "Please. You promised me no more secrets after last year."

Her eyes darted sideways at me, and she scowled. I knew she was surprised I'd brought it up when it had been the longstanding, unspoken agreement that it would never be spoken of again.

Desperate times...

"It's not really a secret, and it's definitely not mine," she said after a moment. "They don't really date anyone, they just both sleep around a lot." She said it with a forceful casualness, and I knew it was an awkward conversation to have, but I had to do it.

"Hm..." I said thoughtfully. It wasn't surprising, given who their father was. Ted had that reputation from the time we were preteens, and I very much suspected the boys had followed in his footsteps in every way. "Well, I guess the reason I asked was because I met a young girl today around your age. Enzo's niece, Sophie. Have you met her?"

She continued drying the dish, but I sensed the hesitation. I knew the answer before she'd given it, but to my surprise, she said, "No, I don't think so. Doesn't ring a bell."

"Are you sure?" I asked, turning off the water after I'd rinsed the final dish. "She's your age, blonde. A bit shorter than you. She said she was here last summer. Surely you saw her around."

"I said I don't know her, Mom." She huffed, opening the cabinet in front of her and putting the mug away before taking the glass baking dish I was holding out to her.

"You're not lying to me, are you? I need you to tell me if you know her."

"Why do you care? What's so special about her?"

"I'm worried about her." I paused, waiting, but she didn't say anything, so I added, "So, do you know her or not?"

"I already told you I didn't. Why are you worried about her? She's fine. Why are you suddenly concerned with who the stupid Dupont brothers are dating?"

"Because the girl was acting strangely today, and I'd seen her talking to Stephanie Dupont just before. They were talking about the boys. I don't trust them, you know that."

She put the baking dish into the cabinet and turned to face me. "So?"

"So, I need to know if there's something going on with them."

"Why do you need to know? What are you going to do?"

"I don't know what I'm going to do, but at the very least, I could warn Enzo to keep an eye on her."

"Can't you just do that regardless? Why do you even care if I know her? If she's around Dom and Raf, she needs to be careful, we both know that."

"Why are you avoiding the question? Do you or do you not recognize her from last summer?"

Her shoulders stiffened and she pressed her lips together, inhaling. "Fine, Mom. Yes, I know her. I saw her around a few times last summer."

"With the Duponts? At their house?"

"Around, Mom." She groaned. "Can we please stop talking about this?"

"If something happened—"

"She was there, yes. I saw her at their house a few times."

"Who was she there to see?"

She chewed her bottom lip. "I don't—" Before she could answer, I heard a rap at the door, and we froze.

A cold chill slipped down my spine and I held up a finger toward her. "Wait here. We aren't finished with this conversation."

With that, I dried my hands on the legs of my pants and made my way toward the door, tossing my hair back over my shoulder. When I pulled it open, Enzo was there, his face ashen, expression grim.

"Enzo, what is—"

"Is Jude home? He's not answering his cell."

"He's..." I heard the water running overhead. "In the shower, sounds like. Do you need me to get him out?"

He nodded, gripping the doorframe. "He needs to come quickly."

"Come where? What's going on?" I tried to maintain my composure, wringing my hands together in front of my waist.

"To the lake, on this side of the bridge. They've found something."

My blood ran cold, my vision tunneling as I tried to process it all and keep my thoughts straight. *No. No. No.* "Found what? What did they find?"

"I, um... A couple of kids were down there playing. They..." He swallowed, his hands trembling. "They found a body, Michelle."

"A bod—"

"*Yes.* They need Jude down there. Please get him now."

CHAPTER TWENTY-THREE

ENZO

I followed Jude's squad car toward the lake, my mind racing with worry and fear. Was it the car Stephanie had seen? Had there really been a crash into the lake and I'd talked her out of reporting it?

Truth be told, I hadn't even thought about it. I'd been so preoccupied with keeping her quiet, keeping people from searching the lake and discovering my secret, I'd never even thought about the person who might've really crashed or why Stephanie had been so willing to change her story.

We pulled up at the lakeside, farther down than the crash site, near the bridge, where a group of teens stood, water-logged and wrapped up in thick, gray blankets. The deputy sheriff, Henry Rodriguez, was talking to the teens while another officer was working to get the area taped off.

As I got out of my car, Jude put a hand up, stopping me. "You have to wait here," he said firmly, crossing under the tape and hurrying toward Rodriguez, his hair still wet from the shower he'd just taken.

Near the edge of the water, there were more people—

EMTs and police officers. I tried to see past them, understand what they were looking at, though the crowd and the dim lighting from the setting sun kept me from seeing anything.

Jude reached the teens, lowering his head slightly as Rodriguez said something in his ear. He looked toward the water, then back to me, his expression dark.

Had they found it?

My breathing grew shallow, my heart pounding in my chest as I felt my knees going weak.

No.

No.

No.

No.

I tried to think, tried to come up with a plan, an explanation. Something that would make sense. Something that would clear my name.

Just then, one of the officers near the water called out and Jude turned toward him, rushing forward. As he approached, the crowd parted, making way for him to stand, which gave just enough space for me to see what they'd found.

It was hard to make out in the evening light, shadows and darkness forcing me to take an extra second to make sense of the sight. First, my eyes took in the blonde hair, darker from the water, then the red, stringy blood mixed into the hair at the roots near her temple. I felt bile rising in my throat as I shook my head, squinting my eyes.

Please. No. It wasn't possible. Was I seeing things? Were my eyes playing tricks on me?

Jude looked back at me once more, a confirmation in his shadowy eyes. He shook his head, a soft, apologetic gesture.

It wasn't what I'd thought, but it was worse. I felt my knees give out with no warning, and I slammed to the ground, the superficial pain no comparison to the agony tearing through my insides.

Oh, Sophie, no. I'm so sorry.

CHAPTER TWENTY-FOUR

STEPHANIE

When I awoke, I stared at the text message on my phone from Mel down at dispatch.

Did you hear? They found a body.

I also had five missed calls from Enzo.

I called him back, but he didn't pick up, so I replied to the text from Mel straightaway. I waited, staring at the phone. I was supposed to be going into work, but how could I with that bombshell? Why wasn't she answering me? How was I supposed to take that? Was it Ted? Had they found him? *Who* had found him? Where?

My mind raced with possibilities, each one worse than the last. But, with no answers, I was forced to examine every worst-case scenario. I jumped out of bed, rushing down the hall to check the boys' rooms. To my relief, they were both safely in their beds. When I'd gone to sleep, Dominic had just arrived home, and I'd planned to talk to them both about the situation with Sophie first thing in the morning.

Now, none of that seemed to matter. Not when I was attempting to prepare myself to deliver the news I knew would destroy them. How could anyone prepare for that?

I cursed under my breath as I checked the phone. Next, I tried to call Mel, but the call went straight to voicemail, which meant she was sleeping.

Maybe it had been a mistake. Maybe it had nothing to do with me. Why wasn't she texting me back?

I needed answers, and I couldn't wait any longer. With no other choice, I slid my phone into my pocket, leaving the house and jogging across the cul-de-sac to the one house, the one person I would've preferred to never ask for information.

But if anyone in Southwest Acres would have it, Michelle Rivera would.

I knocked on the door, praying she was awake already. To my great relief, she answered almost immediately, as if she'd been waiting for me. Her face was pale, her lips parted, and I realized then it hadn't been me she'd hoped to see.

"Hi," she said, obviously confused.

"They found a body," I said.

She nodded slowly. "I know that... How do *you* know that?"

It didn't matter. Nothing mattered except getting an answer. "Was it Ted?" I asked, tears stinging my eyes. I'd thought about this moment so many times over the years, so sure that when I found out where he'd gone, what had happened to him, I wouldn't let it affect me. But to know he may not have run away after all, to know I'd been so angry when, in fact, he hadn't left me at all, but been hurt—been *killed*—instead, it would destroy me.

I shook the thought away. I couldn't go there right now. I needed answers, and I needed them from the woman standing in front of me.

Her brow furrowed, her expression unreadable. Suspicion, maybe? "Why would you ask that?"

"It was, wasn't it?" I felt a cool tear glide down my cheek, but I couldn't move to dry it. "It was him. Oh my god, what am I going to tell the boys?"

Slowly, she shook her head. "It wasn't Ted, Stephanie. It was..." She froze, looking over my shoulder. I followed her gaze, spying Jenn zipping past on her morning walk, pushing her granddaughter in a stroller while talking on the Bluetooth piece in her ear. She waved at us happily, unaware of the dark discussion happening just feet from her. "Come inside," Michelle said under her breath. "But be quiet, Caroline's still asleep."

I couldn't think, couldn't contemplate, so I did as I was told, still processing her words. It wasn't Ted. They hadn't found him. He wasn't dead.

But if not Ted, then who could it have been?

Whose body had been found?

She shut the door behind me and studied me with the same quiet apprehension she'd had when she opened the door. "How did you know they found a body? Did Enzo tell you?"

Her question caught me off guard, and it took me a half second to form an answer. "Enzo? No. One of the girls at dispatch... Wait, does Enzo know? He called me last night, but I missed it."

She nodded stiffly toward the kitchen, leading me in that direction. When we arrived, she dragged one of the barstools around the island so she could sit across from me.

Once I'd sat, she folded her hands in front of her. "I shouldn't be telling you this. Jude could lose his job."

"Please, Michelle... I, if it was Ted, I just need to know."

"I've already told you it wasn't Ted. Why do you think it would be him? He ran away, didn't he? Isn't that what you've been saying all this time? I know it's what you told Jude you believe happened."

"It is what I've been saying, yes," I said. "That's what I

believe, but I don't know that for sure. Obviously, no one does. When I'd heard they found a body, that was immediately where my mind went. I always wonder, even if I think I know..."

She was still, watching me. "It wasn't Ted," she said finally, her tone calming, affirmative. I believed her.

"You're sure?" I was hesitant to feel relief. "Do they know who it was?"

"They know it wasn't him." She paused. "They found the body near the lake."

"The lake?" I took a long, deep breath. *What if...*

"Mhm. Do you think it might've been the person you saw crash into it Tuesday morning?" she asked, one brow raised.

I swallowed. "No, no. It couldn't have been."

"Because you didn't see anyone that night, did you?"

"I told Jude I-I don't know what I saw. There was a light and—"

"You're lying." There was no question in her voice. No hesitancy. She was sure. She knew I'd lied, but she didn't know why. She couldn't.

"I'm not lying, Michelle. Why would you say such a thing?"

"If you really saw something, you wouldn't have changed your story. I think you secretly wanted them to search the lake for some reason. What I don't know is why you changed your mind."

I felt the heat rush to my face. "No. That's ridiculous. I'd never do that. I thought I saw something, but once I'd thought about it more, I realized it must've been my exhaustion. As more time passes, I'm positive there was nothing there. Besides, my boys have been through enough. The idea of dragging them through another investigation when we've only just slowed down from Ted's... I couldn't bear it. I was protecting them more than anything, and Jude understood that."

"We do what we can to protect our children, don't we?" Her sentence carried weight, an accusation. What was she talking about? What did she know?

"I'd do anything to protect them. Same as any mother."

"You should go home, Stephanie. Be with your boys."

"What? Why?" She stood, dismissing me, and panic took hold. I couldn't leave without knowing what they'd found. If not Ted, then who? *"Please. Please just tell me."* I began to sob then, unable to control myself any longer. I needed answers. "Please, Michelle."

"Why should I? It wasn't Ted, so why do you care? Why should I risk my husband's job to tell you anything?" She turned away from me, walking to the sink and filling a glass of water. She didn't bother to offer me one.

My shoulders slumped and I hung my head. It was true. There was no reason, she owed me nothing, but I couldn't move. I couldn't leave that spot, not when all of my secrets were too soon going to be revealed. "I had to protect them," I sobbed.

"What?" She stopped in her tracks on her way back. "Protect who?"

"My boys."

"What are you talking about?"

"They're good boys, Michelle. They're just teenagers. I'm their mother. I had to protect them."

"What did they do?" She was calm, watching me closely, but there was no true surprise in her tone.

"I tried to raise them right, to teach them to be respectful and kind, but something changed a few years ago and I can't fix it. I don't know what he did, I just—"

My phone rang, interrupting the conversation, and I pulled it out. *Thank God.*

"It's Enzo." I read his name on the screen, swiping my finger across it and placing it to my ear. "Hello?"

"I need you." He was crying, his words coming out in short gasps.

"What's wrong?" I shot up from my barstool, moving toward the door with Michelle close behind me. "I'm so sorry I missed your calls last night. What is it? What's going on?"

"It's Sophie," he choked out, the words stopping me in my tracks. *Sophie.* His niece. The Tuesday girl. "She's…dead."

No.

"What do you mean? *How?* Where are you? Where are you?" I held the phone tight to my ear in the hallway, listening closely. I could hear others talking, but he wasn't responding. Not to me anyway.

"I'll be right there," he told someone.

"Enzo? What's going on?"

With no answer, the call ended, leaving me with more questions and no answers. No answers except one.

"It was Sophie," I said, and when I turned around, Michelle's lips were pressed together, a silent confirmation that did nothing to calm my worst fears.

CHAPTER TWENTY-FIVE

MICHELLE

"It was Sophie," Stephanie said, her eyes searching mine for an answer. "She's the one they found. The…the body."

I nodded slowly, searching hers just the same. Did she know? Did she know everything?

"Yes," I said finally.

"She…drown?"

"They haven't identified her cause of death," I said. I knew what Jude had told me, that there was blunt force trauma to her head, but they didn't yet know whether that had killed her before the water. Either way, I wouldn't tell Stephanie. I still didn't know whether I could trust her. In fact, most assuredly I knew I couldn't.

"Enzo needs me," she said, her eyes haunted and wild. "Is he at the lake?"

Before I could answer her question, I had plenty of my own. "Wasn't one of your boys dating Sophie?"

She blinked out of her trance, narrowing her gaze at me. "What? Why would you ask me that?"

"I overheard you two talking about it yesterday at the social. I wasn't eavesdropping, I just walked past when you were by Henry's house. Sounded like something had really upset you both."

She swallowed, composing herself and crossing her arms. "Well, if you heard that, why would you need to ask?"

"Because it looked like Dominic was with a different girl yesterday, and I didn't see Rafael with her either. Teenagers do break up now and again. I thought they may be upset to hear this happened, *if* they are still together." I tried to seem casual and hoped it was working. "They've been through so much already, haven't they, like you said."

"My sons don't talk to me about their dating life, as you can imagine, so I can't speak to who they're seeing or not seeing. I asked her about it because I'd seen her around. But none of that matters. What matters right now is that I get to Enzo. Do you know where he is, or don't you?"

"He's at the lake," I said finally. "I'd imagine they're waiting for the divers to start their search now that it's daylight."

"Divers?" Her eyes widened. "For what?"

"Yes, they're having to bring in a team to use sonar to look for the car you saw." I forced out a steady breath. She couldn't see how shaken I felt. If I could control nothing else, I would control my image.

"But I didn't see a car. I told Jude I was mistaken," she said, her eyes wide with fear. "And Sophie was alive since that night anyway."

"Yes, I know, but she didn't arrive in a car, to everyone's knowledge. Enzo said her car is missing, and because of the suspicious circumstances around her death, they're trying to learn more about her activities between when she left home and when she arrived here. Apparently, she'd run away." I raised my eyebrows. "Izzy must be so devastated."

If I wasn't so terrified, I'd likely be reveling in the over-flow of gossip and scandal. Had she been on drugs? What was she running from? There was so much we still didn't know.

Stephanie shook her head. "B-but they can't... Why would they? I've said I...I was wrong. I didn't see a car that night. I'm sure of it. I was just tired. They shouldn't waste their time."

"Well, I'm not sure what to tell you. You can try to stop them if you hurry. Maybe you can talk to the police, but I don't know. Jude doesn't think it'll do any good. Now that a body's involved, they've had to bring in the homicide department from the state. There's nothing he can do, and Henry had already mentioned your statement to them, and that it may somehow be connected to this. Jude told them everything, about you being tired and realizing that wasn't what you saw, but, with this discovery, they're going to search anyway. Talk about a waste of tax dollars." I scoffed, rolling my eyes and hoping she wouldn't see the worry I was sure would be etched on my face.

Without another word, she spun around, moving away from me and grabbing at the door handle. She rushed out the door, across the subdivision, and into her yellow Jeep. Moments later, I saw it pulling out of the drive and I let my shoulders drop for the first time. Panic began to set in. We had to do something, but there was nothing to do.

For both our sakes, I hoped she could convince them she'd been wrong, convince them to stop the search, but I knew from the helpless tone Jude had conveyed over the phone, the effort was likely futile.

They were going to search the lake.

And I had a feeling all our secrets would soon be revealed.

CHAPTER TWENTY-SIX

ENZO

I had no idea how long it would take to search our seven-acre lake, but at the first signs of daylight, the divers had begun to arrive, carrying various pieces of equipment that they'd been loading up into boats.

Jude had told me at some point throughout the night that I should go home. They'd be taking Sophie's body to the coroner's office and there was nothing else I could do there, but I couldn't leave. I couldn't bring myself to leave without a better understanding of what happened.

After that, he stayed away, no longer providing me with updates, and eventually, as the divers started loading into the boats, an officer I didn't know approached me and moved me across the road, far enough back I could no longer see the lake at all.

As I heard the boats rev up, I knew the search of Lake Guinevere had officially begun, and the sinking feeling I'd had in my stomach for some time only grew worse.

An ambulance had arrived a while ago, but I hadn't seen it depart yet. Sophie was still there. What was left of her. The body, not the soul. From where I sat, I could only catch glimpses of lights and sirens as more and more people arrived. Soon, the news would begin covering what had happened. I sat still, running through everything in my head. I needed to call Izzy and tell her about Sophie—should've done that hours ago—but how would I ever bring myself to do it? I'd asked Jude to let me break the news, but the idea gutted me. I couldn't bear the thought of destroying my sister's life, and I knew that's what I would be doing.

I was supposed to protect her. Sophie had been in my care, and I'd let this happen.

On top of that, I knew my time was coming. If my sister hating me, never forgiving me, wasn't enough, there was also the very real possibility that, upon their search of the lake, the police would find my secret. My truth would be brought to light, and I'd be placed in prison.

I'd tried to call Stephanie that morning, hoping to get a goodbye in, maybe even a chance to explain before they took me, but that was when they'd made me get off the phone to move back away from the scene. I needed to call her back, but I was having a rough time processing everything that was happening.

This was really it for me, wasn't it?

There was still a chance, I supposed, they wouldn't find it. But what were the odds? How good a chance did I have? With the technology they were bringing in, I feared I had no chance at all.

I heard shouting in the distance but couldn't make out anything that was happening. The officer who'd moved me away sat just a few feet from me, staring into the distance silently. Every once in a while, the radio on his shoulder would buzz with quick, indecipherable speech. Soon enough, the town would know what had happened and I'd be joined by dozens of other onlookers, hoping to get a sense of what had happened.

I saw movement in the distance and watched the ambulance turn down the street and drive away without a siren. That would be Sophie. I knew it was coming. I knew they'd be taking her away to get a better understanding of what had happened, but for some reason, seeing that and knowing she was being taken away from me in more ways than one, devastated me. I felt the pain, fresh and on fire once again as it washed over me. I just wanted to be with her. I just wanted this to all be over.

I needed to follow her. I couldn't stay here any longer. She shouldn't be alone.

I stood, drying my eyes and pulling my keys from my pocket. "You can't go back down there," the officer said, calling out to stop me.

"I'm just going to get my car. I need to follow that ambulance. It's my niece." Had I already told him that? I couldn't remember. Everything over the last few hours felt fuzzy.

"You can't get to your car right now. They want everyone a hundred yards from the lake. You'll have to call someone for a ride or wait until they clear the area."

"How long will that take?"

He shrugged, unfazed. "Won't know for a while."

"How the hell is that okay?" I exploded, anger radiating through me.

"Listen, I get that you're upset, but this is an active crime scene—"

"Upset doesn't begin to—"

"*Enzo?*"

I spun around at the sound of my name. Stephanie was there, the window of her Jeep rolled down. I hadn't heard her pull up, so preoccupied with my grief, but as she shut the vehicle off, I ran around to the passenger side of it, feeling so grateful to see her.

"We need to get to the hospital. Did you pass an ambulance on your way here?"

"I saw one, yes," she said seriously. "It was crossing the bridge."

"Follow it." I buckled in and she started the Jeep instantly, following my instructions.

"What's going on?" she asked with tears in her eyes, her hands gripping the steering wheel.

"They aren't telling me anything, but they just took Sophie—" I cut myself off with a sob.

"She's…she was in the ambulance I passed?"

I nodded.

"Did they tell you what happened to her?"

"They won't talk to me. No one will tell me anything. But there was blood…" I touched my head where I'd seen the blood, and she reached over, squeezing my hand.

"I'm so sorry, Enzo. What can I do?"

"I don't know," I said, trying to calm myself down. I used my shoulder to dry a tear from my chin. "I need to call my sister. I need to figure out what they're going to do with her body. We need to make arrangements. I'm sure she'll want her to have a funeral back home with her friends…" I couldn't think. Couldn't focus. There was too much. This was all just too much.

"Okay, one step at a time. I can call Isabel for you," she said hesitantly. "If you want."

"No, it should come from me."

"Are they…are they searching the lake?"

I gave a motion that was somewhere between a headshake and a nod. "Yeah. Yeah, there are so many people out there. I don't really understand it. They found her. What are they even looking for at this point? They won't tell me anything, not even Jude."

"I'm sure it'll all be okay..." She didn't sound sure, but I wasn't in the mood to contradict her.

"Thank you for coming."

"Of course, Enzo."

After that, we both fell quiet for a while, riding out the remainder of the ride in heavy silence. I knew both our minds must be racing. An hour later, we were pulling into the hospital parking lot when she let out a sob and I jerked my head to look at her. Why was she crying?

"What is it?"

"I need to tell you something."

My heart skipped a beat, my throat suddenly dry.

"I know this isn't the right time, but it's going to come out and it should come from me." She pulled into a parking space, staring at me with a haunted expression.

"What is it?"

Before she could answer, I felt my phone buzzing in my pocket. Though I desperately didn't want to, I pulled it out. "Hang on, this is Jude now."

I put the phone to my ear. "Hello?"

"Are you still here?"

"I'm on my way to the hospital to see Sophie."

"I'm so sorry, Enzo. About everything. Please tell Izzy that for me too."

"What happened to her? Do you know? I kept trying to flag you down, but—"

"Look—" He cut me off. "I don't have much time to talk, but I wanted to let you know we found something else."

"What is it?"

He hesitated. "We found a gun, Enzo. At the bottom of the lake."

My blood ran ice cold, and I knew what was coming next. "A gun? Sophie was..."

He lowered his voice. "She wasn't shot, no. But the wound

on her head could've been caused by the butt of the gun. We haven't confirmed that yet. Actually, the reason I'm calling is that I recognize the make and model. It's a Smith & Wesson Model 65 in .357 Magnum."

I felt my chest tighten.

Here it comes.

"The same gun that killed Leslie."

I nodded, forcing a response. *"What?* What does that mean? How is it possible?*"*

"Yeah, I'm not sure yet, so I'm doing this as a courtesy. They haven't put the link together to Leslie's case, but once they run it in the system, they will. I need you to come down to the station for questioning. I know you were planning to go to the hospital, but can you meet me at the station in an hour instead? So we can get it out of the way."

I nodded slowly, barely able to squeak out an answer. "Yes."

"Okay. I'll, uh, I'll see you soon."

With that, we ended the call and I looked at Stephanie, who looked equally terrified. "What did he say?"

"They found a gun."

"What?" Her jaw dropped. "Who, the…"

"The police. The divers." I tapped my phone. "We have to turn around. I have to go down to the station for questioning."

"Questioning? Why? They can't think that you had anything to do with this. You'd never… Jude knows you wouldn't… Enzo, you loved her. We all know that."

"I did." We weren't talking about the same woman, but both sentiments were true. I did love her, regardless of my crime. "Sophie wasn't shot. She was…he said she was hit in the head. But it's…it's the same type of gun that killed Leslie."

Her jaw went slack, her eyes wide with horror. "Oh my

god, Enzo... I—" She didn't seem sure what to say as she shook her head back and forth, her eyes searching mine.

"I'm going to be arrested."

"Why would you say that?" she asked, reaching for my hands. She gathered them in hers. "You didn't do this. I know you're innocent."

"It doesn't matter now. They'll connect the two, if not the three. The gun, my wife, Sophie now... The only link is me."

"No, that's not true. There has to be something else. You were with me most of the day. I can tell them that."

"I wasn't with you the whole day. People saw me at the social, alone. I'd left your house more than an hour before they found her. I won't have you lying for me."

"You didn't do this. I know that. I trust you." She lifted her hands, pressing them to her lips. "Come on, we have to think. The gun wasn't yours, right? You told me before that they cleared all your guns after it happened."

"Yeah, it wasn't mine, but Leslie's dad had one. He gave it to her after he died, but it was stolen before she died, probably years before. I haven't seen it in over a decade."

"Okay, so it was stolen. And you reported it?"

"Yeah, we did. A few months before Leslie died, we were moving stuff around and realized it was missing. We reported it then."

"So, you couldn't have done it. Jude will know that. Whoever stole the gun, whoever killed Leslie, if they used it to kill Sophie, they must've thrown it in the lake afterward. This could all be the same person, but it wasn't you."

"It doesn't matter. They won't have any other suspects. I know how this story plays out, Steph." I leaned forward, pressing my lips to hers. "I'm just glad I got to be with you, *officially*, for at least one day."

When we broke apart, her expression was sad, soft. "There has to be another way."

"Well, if you can think of one, I'm all ears." I laughed dryly, the warmth of it feeling foreign to me. Nothing in me warranted laughter. I was a pit of fear and rage. I was going to jail. My life was over. These were my last moments with the woman I'd risked everything for. "But otherwise, Jude is going to be waiting for us at the station."

"Should we go to the hospital first?"

"No," I said simply. "If I go anywhere but the police station, I don't think I'll ever find the courage to go. If I don't go now, I may never."

"We could run," she said softly. "We could leave now. By the time they realized—"

"You'd leave with me?" I asked her, surprised by the suggestion.

"I could take you somewhere," she said, though she seemed to be trying to convince herself more than me. "Then come back for the boys."

I shook my head, blowing air from my nose. "You have to think of them first. You can't save me from this."

A tear fell down her cheek, and I brushed it away with my thumb. "I love you," I told her, placing my lips where the tear had been.

"I love you, too." She dusted another tear away, and I nodded toward the keys.

"Come on. Don't cry. We should go."

She turned away reluctantly and started the Jeep, looking straight ahead with a locked jaw as she pulled back out of the parking space and drove us toward the station.

We rode the rest of the way in painful silence, our hands locked together tightly, as if we could squeeze tight enough to get ourselves out of this mess.

When we arrived, Jude's car was already there. I turned to her, staring into her eyes one last time. We launched forward, pressing our lips together in a moment of heated passion. I tasted her for what I knew would be the last time.

Then, without warning, I tore myself away from her, opening the door and moving away out of the Jeep, hot, angry tears burning my eyes.

Why now?

Why was this happening now?

I opened the doors to the police station in a daze, moving past Millie at the desk and toward Jude's office. Everything was happening in slow motion as he stood, lifting a hand to lead me into an unfamiliar room.

It wasn't like in the movies. The room wasn't dark with a single, swinging light above our heads. It was small and stale smelling with old, yellowed tile on the floor and wood paneling on the walls. We sat across from each other at a small, metal table and he smiled, but it was forced.

"Thanks for coming down."

"You didn't give me any choice."

He ran his fingers over his upper lip, as if stroking a mustache that wasn't there. "I know you must be a wreck over Sophie, and I know you're dealing with a lot over that, so I promise I'll make this as painless as possible. I just have to get this out of the way or, when they make the connection, they're going to ask why I didn't. It's not like we get a lot of murders here—"

"A surprising amount for a town of this size," I grumbled under my breath.

"So, a case like Leslie's, those details get remembered." He opened an olive green folder in front of him, flipping through papers I couldn't see. "I know your alibi was from a bar in Paducah and you had a receipt to prove you were there, but you paid in cash..."

"Yeah, you said that was fine."

"It was. It...it is, it's just—"

The door burst open, interrupting us, and Stephanie was suddenly in the room, her eyes bloodshot, cheeks red.

"Wait! Jude, it wasn't Enzo!" she cried, catching herself on the table.

We stood, startled by the rambunctious entrance, and Jude lowered his head, trying to look her in the eye. "Stephanie? What's going on? Are you okay?"

She panted, holding her chest as she spoke through her tears and heavy breaths. "It wasn't Enzo. You have to listen to me. He didn't kill his wife, and he didn't kill Sophie."

"What are you talking about?" we asked at the same time. What was she saying?

"Do you know who it was?" Jude added.

"Yes," she said, shaking her head slowly, her chin quivering. "It was him. I didn't want to believe it, but it has to be him. I'm so sorry. God, I'm so sorry."

He took her shoulders in his hands, trying to calm her down so we could make sense of the rambling. "What? Slow down. I'm not understanding. Who are you talking about? It was who?"

She brushed her tears away a final time and then, instead of looking at Jude as she gave her answer, she looked at me. In her eyes, there was an apology. "Ted. It was Ted."

CHAPTER TWENTY-SEVEN

STEPHANIE

Jude stood in front of me, his eyes filled with disbelief, but I could only look at Enzo, could only take in the pain and heartbreak on his face. I should've told him sooner, but I couldn't bring myself to do it. I couldn't bring myself to tell him the truth, to break his heart, because I knew he'd never look at me the same.

He'd never forgive me.

Never respect me.

I'd sooner lose everything than his respect, but I wouldn't lose him. Enzo didn't deserve to go down for my husband's crimes, and certainly not to protect myself.

"What do you mean *it was Ted?*" Jude asked slowly, speaking as if he thought I'd lost my mind. "Ted's gone."

"I thought so, too, but he wasn't when Leslie died. He killed her before he took off. And I'm sure he's back now, and that means he's probably the one who killed Sophie, too."

"You know this for sure?" Jude asked. "You know that Ted killed Leslie? How?"

"You don't have to do this," Enzo said, shaking his head.

"I do," I said firmly. "I've hidden the truth for so long

because he said he'd kill me if I ever told, but now, he's gone. I should've come forward ages ago, but I didn't know where he was. I didn't know if he'd come back for me. I was just trying to protect the boys." I was crying then, tears pouring down my cheeks as my sobs shook my shoulders. "I'm so sorry, Enzo."

Jude gestured toward his chair, a hand on my shoulder as he led me to it. "I need you to sit down and tell me everything." He rested one elbow in the other hand, his fist pressed into his lips. "So, Ted *told* you he killed Leslie?"

I thought then, trying to piece together my story. I'd never planned to tell this story. I never wanted them to look at me the way I knew they would, but I had no choice. I had to save Enzo, consequences be damned.

"Not at first. Not when it happened. But…" I shivered, running my hands over my arms to warm them. "Leslie knew something about Ted. A secret."

"What secret?" Jude demanded, stopping in his tracks.

"I don't know exactly, but I assume it had something to do with the fact that he was sleeping with some of his students."

"He *what?*" Enzo's face wrinkled with confusion. "*Ted?*"

I nodded. "He never talked to me about it, but I caught him in our house one day with a girl…" My body tensed at the memory. Walking into our bedroom to find her in our bed, Ted half dressed. "One of his students."

The air was sucked out of the room, both men hanging on to my every word.

"He told me it was the first time. The girl was eighteen and there was nothing I could do by telling anyone, except to stir up drama and cost Ted his job. We went to counseling, and I thought it had helped. I thought it was just the one girl—"

"But it wasn't?"

"I don't know for sure, but no, I assume now that he was lying to me. Like he lied about everything else."

"Did you talk to the parents of the girl?" Jude asked. "Did you *do* anything?"

Guilt weighed heavy in my stomach. "No. I should have, I know. But I was embarrassed. Ashamed. The girl was there willingly... I know that's no excuse, she was young and he was in a position of power, but I couldn't feel anything for her other than rage. Fury. I wanted to leave him, but he said he'd take the boys away. They were old enough to choose, and they would've chosen him, we both knew it. When I threatened to tell, he said he'd sooner kill me than have anyone find out the truth. He cared about his reputation too much. There was something in his eyes that night..." I stared into the distance, the memory haunting me. "He was telling the truth. If I'd said anything, he would've killed me. I can't explain how I know it, but I do. I did. He wasn't lying about that."

"I don't understand," Enzo said after a moment. "What does any of this have to do with Leslie?"

"I think she found out what was happening. Maybe she caught him, maybe a student told her, I'm not sure, but what I do know is that Ted had begun to watch your house carefully in the weeks and months before she died. When I'd ask about work, he always had a complaint about her—how she was running her classroom, how much the students hated her. I thought it was just silly coworker drama, but the day she died, when the sound of the gunshot woke me up, he wasn't home. I called and called, but he didn't answer. The police"—I looked at Jude—"you were there so quickly, but not quick enough to catch him. When he got home a few hours later and I told him what had happened, he didn't look sorry. In fact, he smirked." I shivered at the thought, the way I'd felt sick to my stomach at the sight of his smile. "He said 'I guess the bitch finally got what she deserved.'"

Enzo put his head into his hands, and I forced myself to look away.

"I wanted to come forward, but I thought I was protecting my family. My boys. I was terrified of what Ted would do if I ever told anyone what I suspected."

"Do you have any reason to believe Ted could've taken the gun from Enzo's house?" Jude asked, looking between us.

"I never saw it, no. Ted wasn't really a gun guy. We didn't have any in our house, but I guess that would make it seem even less likely that it was him. Ted was smart that way."

"He was at my house quite a bit," Enzo said softly, almost as if he was regretting saying it as it left his mouth. "You both were. I can't believe he would steal from me, or that he would hurt her, but he definitely had the chance to take it if he wanted to. I mean, he knew where we kept our guns, where we kept the key to that closet."

Jude nodded. "It's true, I guess, but even if what you're saying is true, even if Ted killed Leslie, he's gone now. No one has heard from him in months. Why would you think he had something to do with Sophie's death?" Jude asked, his voice cool and calm, as if the emotions Enzo and I were feeling couldn't touch him.

"I would've never thought anything about it, but where you found Sophie... It reminded me of a conversation I had with Ted. We were watching something on the news about the investigation into Leslie's death, and he seemed angry. Angrier than normal. I asked him if something was bothering him, and he mumbled something about how the killer should've taken her down to the lake if they didn't want her to be found. He said it was just common sense. Called the killer stupid."

Jude's brow furrowed. Enzo still hadn't looked up.

"It would've been impossible. I was there that night. The entire neighborhood heard the gunfire right away. I was out my door and at Leslie's house in minutes," Jude said.

"I know. I didn't think he was serious at the time. I thought he was just making some sick joke. He always had this dark sense of humor, you remember. But, when they found Sophie at the lake, it just made sense. The lake, Ted, it's all connected… It has to be. He's back, and he was getting rid of his final piece of evidence."

"Final piece of evidence?" Enzo demanded, looking up at me.

I couldn't meet either of their eyes this time. If any part of this held shame for me, it was this. "Sophie spent most of last summer at our house while she was visiting. I was at work, but Ted and the boys were home. I thought she was seeing one of them, the boys, I mean. I'd caught her leaving the house a few times when I'd gotten home earlier than usual. I'd invited her to stay for dinner, but she never wanted to. I didn't know she was your niece, Enzo. I thought she was just a random girl from school."

I inhaled sharply. "In fact, I'd forgotten about her. It was just a few times that we'd run into one another, and not at all since last summer. But then when I met her again on Tuesday with Dominic, I thought she looked familiar, but I couldn't decide why. And then when you told me she was your niece and I talked to her again, hearing her voice, it just all started coming back to me slowly. And last night, when Dom came home, I confronted him about mistreating her, and he said they'd never even slept together. He said he didn't know her that well, that she'd asked him to pick her up and bring her here on Monday. She told him she was supposed to be meeting a friend, but when she got here, they blew her off. But, when I realized they weren't together last summer, I just started to connect all the dots and realize how wrong I was about all of this. I don't think she was with my sons."

I watched their expressions, trying to see if they were piecing it together as I told the story. "I think she was sleeping with my husband, and she didn't know he was missing. I think she came here for him. And I think he either killed her because she wouldn't leave him alone or because she found out the truth about what he did to her aunt."

Jude leaned forward on the table, staring at me. "Do you really think he's capable of what you're accusing him of? Do you believe he could've killed Leslie and Sophie?"

I nodded stiffly, swallowing. "If he thought someone was going to hurt him or his reputation, I believe he would be capable of anything." I swiped away a new tear. "It was why I said I saw a car going into the water that night. It was stupid and I immediately regretted it, but those words, what he said that night, it's haunted me since he disappeared. I know they were spread apart, but there've been a few girls from the town who've disappeared…"

"Laura Dickson and Emily Evans," Jude confirmed. "A few others going back several years. All around the same age, too."

I nodded.

"So, you truly didn't see anything that night?"

"I'm sorry. I didn't want to lie, but I didn't know what else to do. Hearing him say what he had, knowing what I knew about him, it just always made me wonder if he had something to do with their disappearances. And the boys revere their father. They emulate his behavior, and part of me wondered, if he'd done what I thought, if he'd hurt those girls and they could prove it somehow, if there were consequences for his behavior, would they realize that they're idolizing the wrong man? That the person they're aspiring to be just like was really a criminal."

"So, wait, you're saying you think he may have killed those girls and…what? Put them in the lake?"

"I don't know, Jude," I told him firmly. "Honestly, I don't. I hope you don't find anything at all. I hope I'm wrong and that this nagging feeling in my gut is just there, but I hoped when they didn't find a car, they might find something else. Something to give me peace over hating him so badly."

"Why didn't you come to me?" Enzo asked. "Why didn't you tell me you were scared? I would've taken care of you."

"Or me?" Jude asked. "You could've come to any of us."

"And you would've believed me? You were all friends with Ted in high school. For all I knew, you wouldn't have believed me and you would've told him what I said."

"You knew I wouldn't do that," Enzo said.

"No, I didn't. That's the point. I thought I knew my husband. I thought he was a good man. I wanted so badly to believe he wasn't capable of anything like this that I convinced myself I was going crazy, that I'd fallen out of love with him and was just trying to find a way out. When you love someone, you don't believe they could be capable of something so evil. So, what if I told you and you didn't believe me? Or you, Jude? It was too much of a risk."

"So, why now?" Jude asked. "Why now if you believe he's back? You could be in danger again."

"Because Enzo can't go to jail for what Ted did. Even if it puts me in danger, I can't let him go to jail without telling you what I know." I met Enzo's eye. "I had to try."

"And you're not just telling me this to protect Enzo now, right? You're not lying about it? Because finding the murder weapon there, it does add clout to your story, to Ted's guilt. But if I go out there and make this phone call, ask them to search for bodies—bones—and we find something, your secret won't stay a secret. Even if we find nothing, the town will know. So you need to make sure that's what you want."

I nodded without hesitation. "They're going to crucify me, but I have to do the right thing. For once in my life."

He pressed his lips together, nodding slowly. "I just need to ask you one more question."

"Anything." I felt Enzo's hands grip mine as we waited for Jude to go on.

"I have to ask you, given what you've told me, did you kill your husband to protect yourself?"

"I… *What?*"

"After learning what he did, what you suspected he did, it would be understandable. There's a chance we could talk to the DA about a deal."

"I didn't kill Ted," I said, my voice shaking. "As much as I wanted to some days, I could never have gone through with it. I'm not a killer."

His nod was apprehensive, and I knew he didn't believe me. "Okay, I need to make a call." Without another word, he backed out of the room, already on his cell phone, and I turned to Enzo.

"I'm sorry."

He kissed my hands. "Don't ever apologize for what you just did. I love you for saving me."

I smiled at him sadly, glad to hear he didn't blame me for keeping the secret for so long. I just had to hope I actually *had* saved him. Otherwise, this would've all been for nothing.

CHAPTER TWENTY-EIGHT

MICHELLE

When Jude finally arrived home after midnight on Monday, it had been more than two full days since I'd last seen him. When cases were particularly hard, he sometimes stayed at the station, but with everything going on, all the worry and fear, his absence felt particularly hard this time.

His shoulders were slumped, his footsteps heavy as he made his way into the house, then into the room. I was on the kitchen floor, scrubbing the front of our cabinets with a soapy sponge to keep myself busy. I dropped the sponge in the bucket next to me and stared at him with a sigh.

I'd wait for him to speak, to deliver whatever bad news was undoubtedly coming.

"They found bodies."

"Oh my god. Bodies, plural?"

"Bones, more like."

I stood, wiping my hands across the seat of my pants. I felt as if I were going to be sick. "Okay. Do they know whose?"

"Not yet. They'll start putting them together. Matching them to dental records. It could take a while, but they'll figure it out eventually."

"Are they done with the search?"

"I think so," he said, grabbing a soda out of the refrigerator. "They may head back out tomorrow, but I don't think they believe there's anything else to find."

"But who else could've been there? Are they from a long time ago? Could you tell what happened to them?"

He shook his head. "We don't know anything yet. Some of them could've been there for a few decades, maybe. Some of them less."

"And did they find…"

"I wasn't there, but I'd say so. Yes. It's not a big lake. He wouldn't have been down deep."

I swallowed, trying and failing to process. My worst fears were now a reality. What were we going to do about it?

"There's still nothing connecting us to him. Not really. They may never look at us. We'll just… We'll have to prepare Caroline."

He was still, his gaze locked on nothing in particular as he appeared lost in thought. After a moment, he inhaled sharply. "There's something else I need to tell you."

I felt my insides liquefy, my body ice cold. "Something else?"

"We found the murder weapon from Leslie Barone's murder."

I gasped. "What?"

"It was in the lake. The gun belonged to Leslie's father. The one Enzo had reported missing before the murder."

My eyes widened. "Does Enzo know?"

"We had to bring him down. He would've had access to it."

"But he wouldn't... He didn't *kill* her." My breathing caught. "Enzo's our friend."

"Ted was our friend, too," he said simply.

I was silent for a moment. *Point taken.* "So, what does it mean? What did he say?"

"Well, he didn't have a chance to say much, because when we brought him in, Stephanie showed up and gave a confession of her own."

"Stephanie? What do you mean? What did she confess?"

"There were others, Michelle." His eyes drilled into mine then, the truth there plain as day. "Others besides Caroline. If we hadn't... If she hadn't... The bodies in the lake. I think... He was going to kill her." He looked as if he were going to be sick.

I put a hand to my chest. I didn't want to go back to that night. Desperately, I didn't, but at his words, I had no choice. Suddenly, I was reliving the night four months ago that had changed everything.

The darkest night of my life.

THE PHONE RANG *out in the dead of night. I ignored it, thinking it was Jude's phone, another call he'd have to run out to respond to. But he hadn't moved.*

The ringing ended, and I began to drift off to sleep, finding the solace of my dreams once more. Within seconds, I heard the noise again. This time, I lifted my head off my pillow as I realized it wasn't Jude's phone at all, but mine.

My phone never rang at night, so if someone was calling, it couldn't be good news. My mind immediately went to my parents, my sister, my nieces... When I lifted the phone and stared at the photo of Caroline from the night of her seventeenth birthday, smiling up at us from behind glowing candles, my heart sank.

Why was she calling me from her room? Was she sick? I sat up in bed, sliding my finger across the screen and putting the phone to my ear.

"Baby? What's wrong?"

"Mom?" came the immediate response. She was crying. I rubbed my eyes, looking at the clock. It was just after two in the morning.

"What's going on, Caroline?" I was up out of bed, making my way toward the door. "Where are you? Are you calling me from your room?"

I knew from the sounds of the wind that the answer was no, but nothing made sense to me in my half asleep state.

"Mom, I'm sorry. I messed up. I'm so sorry." I could barely understand her through the sound of her tears, but suddenly, panic was overwhelming me.

What had she done?

Where was she?

What had happened?

Was she hurt?

"Caroline, where are you? What's going on?"

"You're going to kill me. I'm so sorry." I could hardly hear her, her voice muffled, and I pictured her resting her face in her hands as she often did when crying. "I don't know what to do. I didn't know who else to call."

"Where are you?" I repeated more firmly. I moved back toward our bed, jostling my husband awake. "Where are you, Caroline? Stop crying and talk to me."

"I'm at the lake," she said with a long, ragged breath. "I'm down by the lake with Mr. Dupont."

The sentence came out of nowhere, shocking me completely. Why on earth would she be with Ted Dupont in the middle of the night? I had half a mind to call up our old friend and yell at him. But still, there was a bit of relief, knowing she was with him. Knowing she was safe. Then there was anger. She was supposed to be in her bedroom. She was supposed to be waking up for school in just a few hours.

"Put him on the phone, please."

"I can't," she said softly.

"You can't what?"

"I can't put him on the phone." She was sobbing again.

She'd lied.

"Who are you really with, Caroline? You can tell me. I just want you to be safe. Have you been drinking? Do you need us to come pick you up?"

"Yes," came the soft, muffled response.

"Where are you exactly?"

"By the lake," she said again. "By the bridge."

"Okay, stay right there." Jude had finally begun to wake up, his eyes still heavy with sleep as he stared up at me. "Your father and I will be there in just a few minutes, okay?"

"Please hurry," she whined, and I ended the call.

"Get dressed," I told my husband. "Your daughter snuck out. We have to go and get her."

"She did what?" he demanded, grabbing for the clothes lying on the floor near the end of the bed, clothes he'd stripped out of just a few hours before. "Is she okay? Where is she?"

"She's by the lake, and she's crying. I'm not sure what happened. We just need to get there."

We were dressed and in the car in minutes. We'd considered taking Jude's cop car, but it seemed safer not to. At the moment, it hadn't seemed wise to let the neighborhood gossips see us down there, but looking back, I wonder if I knew. I wonder if somehow, I just knew whatever Caroline had done, we'd spend the rest of our lives covering it up.

I was angry with her, but terrified too. It wasn't like her. I'm sure most parents would say that about their children, but it truly wasn't like our daughter. She was smart, quiet, and undeniably *focused on school. She'd dated and had friends, but she wasn't a partier. She rarely left the house on Saturday nights and never missed a curfew. So what had happened to change that?*

I knew the answer to that, the only answer there ever was for a teenage girl suddenly acting out of the ordinary: there was a boy.

I never would've guessed, even with her telling me his name, that it was actually a man. Actually our friend.

We arrived at the lake less than twenty minutes later, spying her car parked along the side of the highway. Immediately, I was thankful that no one drove this stretch of road at night, not once the bar had closed down.

We leaped from the car and rushed forward, searching for her. Hers was the only car there, so she was either alone, or had someone who'd ridden with her.

As we moved closer, I saw her dark figure moving in the shadows near the base of the bridge. When she recognized us, she rushed forward, her body shaking as she fell into my arms. I kissed her head, my anger melting away as I held her against my chest. I'd kissed away so many booboos, but I couldn't kiss away heartbreak, no matter how badly I wanted to.

Who is he, *I wondered.* Who'd hurt her so badly? Who had broken my baby's heart?

I held her head between my palms, lowering myself to look into her eyes. "Let's get you home, okay? You can tell us everything there."

"No," she said, pulling away from me.

"Listen to your mother, Caroline," Jude said sternly. "We need to go—"

"We can't go home," she said, shaking her head and glancing behind her. "Not until we..."

"Until we what?" I demanded.

"Is someone here with you?" Jude asked, following her gaze and moving forward to peer around the base of the bridge, the sturdy, concrete piles dug into the earth.

"It's Mr. Dupont," she said again, and finally, what she'd told me truly sank in. "I didn't mean to, I— It was an accident. He was going to hurt me, and I just reacted. I didn't mean to." She was sobbing into my arms again as I looked at Jude with panic, watching him approach the bridge cautiously. When he reached the base, looking at something I couldn't see, I saw him freeze. He stood still for an extra second, then moved forward, disappearing behind the concrete.

"What happened, Caroline? Who was going to hurt you? Where is Ted? Is he here with you?" I knew, but I had to ask. I wanted her to tell me I was wrong, that I had it all wrong.

"I'm pregnant, Momma." Her face was against my chest, her words muffled, but I'd heard all I needed to. Her tears soaked through my shirt as I collapsed onto the ground, holding her tight. "It was an accident. H-he wanted me to get rid of it, but I didn't want to."

"T-Ted?" My vision blurred. My daughter was pregnant? My daughter was having sex? My daughter was having sex with her teacher? Our friend? My daughter was pregnant. Our friend had gotten my daughter pregnant. Our adult friend, her teacher, a man we'd trusted more than anyone else had gotten our child pregnant.

No.

No.

No.

No.

It wasn't possible. She was still a child. She was smart. She knew better.

He knew better. He'd known her since she was a baby. He'd taken care of her as a child. How was this possible?

How was any of this possible?

Before I could respond, Jude was jogging back toward us. Even in the moonlight, I could see the pale shock on his face.

"Go back to the house, Caroline," he said, swiping a tear from his cheek with the back of his hand.

"Daddy, I—"

"I said go," he bellowed.

"Jude—" I tried to calm him.

"We don't have much time," he said, striking up a new sense of panic in me. "Caroline, back to the house. Your mother and I will take care of this."

"Momma, I—"

"Listen to your father," I told her, still trying to process the instruction myself. How were we going to take care of this? How were we going to do anything ever again besides melt right here into the mud? What were our options? Our life had imploded.

Caroline stood, making her way back to the car, casting cautious glances over her shoulder every few steps. Once she was in the car, backing out, the headlights passed over Jude slowly and I saw the blood on his hands, his shirt.

"Oh my God."

"We don't have time for you to panic," he said, the professional, sheriff version of my husband on full display. "Someone could drive down and see us at any time. I need your help."

"What did she do?" I asked, though I wasn't sure I wanted to know. "Is he..."

"He's dead," he said, answering the question I hadn't asked. Couldn't bring myself to ask.

"Are you sure? We could call an ambulance or—"

"He can't be saved." The statement was simple enough, but painful and complicated in my panic-ridden state. How could he not be saved? He had a family. He had a wife. He was our friend. He was—

"She's pregnant, Jude," I said, remembering what she'd told me as we moved closer. "He didn't want her to keep it."

He didn't respond, but as we neared the water's edge, the scene became clear. In the moonlight, I could see Ted's body, his legs in the water, upper half still on the shore. His head had been smashed, *his face a Jackson Pollock painting of dark, oozing blood. Next to him lay a single, fist-sized rock, its point drenched in blood, the outer edges speckled red.*

My knees gave out and I fell to the ground, but Jude pulled me back up. "You can't fall apart right now. We have to get rid of the body."

"Ted's..." I was going to pass out. I was sure of it.

"Yes, Ted's dead. And if we don't get rid of his body, our daughter will go to jail."

The sentence brought me back to reality. I didn't have time to think. Instead, I followed Jude's lead, stuffing our friend's pockets with as many rocks as would fit. When that was done, we pulled him out into the water. Jude moved as far as he could with the body, losing his footing and slipping in more than once. Once we'd moved as far out as we safely could, farther even than I thought we could, Jude let him go, giving the body one final shove.

I caught the glint of his tears in the moonlight as he made his way back to me, and I thought of the many afternoons he'd spent in the garage having a beer with Ted and Enzo, the weekends away, the ball games they'd played in and attended. They had a whole life together, a childhood built together, and we'd just discarded him this way.

But he'd slept with our child.

He'd gotten her pregnant.

He'd snuck her out of our house and asked her to have an abortion.

He'd broken our trust in the worst possible way.

I couldn't separate the two in my head. The Ted I loved. The Ted who had attended our Thanksgivings and been Jude's best man, and the Ted who had been a monster.

Back at the shore, we used the water to wash the blood from the earth as much as we could, rinsing the rocks and the mud clean and covering up our shoe prints.

When it was done, we made our way back to the car, wet and muddy. We didn't talk the entire way home, just sat in silence, the weight of what we'd done heavy on our minds. We took off our clothes at home, washing them with Caroline's and using an unhealthy amount of bleach.

Over the next few hours, Caroline told us the whole story. How he'd offered to tutor her in his history class because her grades had started slipping. She was sure she still understood everything, but for whatever reason, she'd begun doing worse and worse on her tests and homework.

He told her she could come by the house and study.

She said the first session went fine.

But each session after, he'd started to make odd comments about how she looked, or to joke about how mature she was for her age or how fast she was growing up. Soon enough, he'd made his first move.

She was shy. He was her teacher and our friend, and she didn't want to make him mad or get into trouble.

She was afraid to tell us, afraid we'd be mad at him, rather than her. And soon, she found herself developing feelings. She thought he cared about her. She thought he loved her.

It was a mistake and she knew it, but she'd never had any true experience with a crush and Ted had manipulated her. He'd betrayed us all.

When she found out she was pregnant, he offered to pay for an abortion, but it wasn't what she wanted. He asked her if they could go for a drive down to the lake that night to talk everything through, and when she hadn't agreed with him about the way forward, he'd lunged for her. She said he'd had his hands around her throat when she reached for the rock.

Like so much else of their relationship, it all happened so fast, and before she knew it, he was dead.

Jude coached her on her story, though I knew it destroyed him— both as a cop, a father, and a friend—to do so. He told her she could

never tell anyone what happened, or anything about their relation-
ship, and that we wouldn't either. We would never speak about that
night again.

And we didn't.

UNTIL NOW.

CHAPTER TWENTY-NINE

ENZO

When the call came on Thursday, I heard the news while sitting at the end of the bed next to Stephanie, her phone on speaker. She hadn't left the room since we'd made it home from the police station, convinced the entire town must hate her.

Maybe they did, it wasn't for me to say. What I knew was that she'd saved me, and for that I would always love her.

I'd spent the week traveling back and forth between my house and hers, between my grieving sister and my grieving love.

"I just heard back from the medical examiner. The report confirms that we found four bodies," Jude was saying.

"Four?"

"Three teenage girls, one adult male."

"Who are they?" I heard her inhale sharply. "An adult male. That isn't possible... It can't be him." She didn't want to believe it, but I saw the acceptance in her eyes, pain and relief swirling around each other as she fought to decide which to feel.

"We've contacted Dr. Getty to get his dental records, as

well as records from any of the girls who have disappeared in the last thirty years or so. I'll let you know more when we find out."

"Thanks," she said, staring at her phone.

"Take care of yourself. I'll be in touch." Seconds later, the call ended and she looked up at me. Her lips were pressed together. I leaned forward, squeezing her hand.

"Are you okay?" I asked. It was a simple, ridiculous question, but I had nothing else for her. What were you supposed to ask in a moment like this?

"What if it's him?" she asked. "What will I tell the boys?"

"You tell them that you love them and that you're here. That you're safe. But you shouldn't worry about it yet. Wait until Jude tells us something. It might not even be him."

"I don't know which possibility I should be more afraid of." She looked down, grasping my hand and rubbing her thumb over my knuckles. "I need you to be honest with me about something."

My stomach clenched. "Anything." *Lie.*

She nodded as she asked. "Did you know? About Leslie? About Ted? About what he was doing? About him threatening me and killing her? Did you kill him to protect me?"

My fingers loosened in her hand. "Where did that even come from?"

"I've just been thinking, and it's a possibility I've considered. You've always taken such good care of me, and I will understand if you did it. Believe me, I'll understand. I just need to know. I need to prepare myself."

I scoffed, cocking my head to the side. "I didn't kill Ted. You know I'm not capable of that. I'd do anything to protect you, but I'm not a monster."

"Do you swear it? Enzo, please don't lie to me. Anything you tell me, I'd never tell a soul."

"I didn't kill him, Stephanie. How can you even ask me that?"

She puffed out a breath of air. "I just had to look you in the eye when you answered me." She hesitated, but I knew there was more she wanted to ask.

"What is it?"

"What about Leslie?"

A wave of cold washed through me. "What about her?"

"Did you kill her?"

"You already said Ted did. Why are you talking like this?"

"I believe Ted did, yes. Everything I told Jude in that room was true, but it was also to save you. I have no proof Ted did anything, other than speculation. So, before we go any further, I need to know, I need to hear it from you that you didn't. We'd been seeing each other for a while at that point, and you wanted to be with me. You talked about us leaving them both, and I kept saying it was too complicated. I said we couldn't be together because of them, no matter what. That I'd never leave Ted and that I couldn't face this town if you left Leslie, or if anyone ever found out about us. It wasn't long after that Leslie died."

My face wrinkled with repulsion. "You really think I could do something like that? You think I'm capable of killing my own wife?"

"You aren't saying no."

"If you honestly believe I'm that kind of man, why would you even bother saving me?"

"Because I love you. And because I don't believe you are, but I have to ask."

"And what about Ted? How do I know *you* didn't kill him?"

"How do I know *you* didn't?" she asked. "I told the police about Ted to protect you, but you need to tell me the truth about everything. And if what you've told me is the complete and total truth, great. But, if not, now's the time to tell me."

Her tone was clipped, and I could hardly hear her over the sound of my heart thudding in my ear. I stood from the bed. "I can't do this right now. I need to go."

"Wait! Don't leave!" she called, but I was already at the door, then out of the room. I had nothing left to say to her.

Not now.

Not when she'd just accused me of...

Exactly what happened.

Not Ted, no. Of that crime, I was completely innocent. But Leslie had to happen. She had to die. She'd told me about Ted and the students, claimed she'd gone to Principal Warner, but no one believed her. People were smitten with Ted. They believed him, took his word over everyone else's. It had been that way in school too, but, to this day, I didn't understand the appeal. Like it or not, though, Ted was charming and he'd always been popular. The students he was sleeping with wouldn't tell the truth, whether because of threats against them or their feelings for him, so it was her word against theirs.

Truth be told, I didn't even know if I believed her, and I was never that big a fan of Ted to begin with. That's how good he was.

She was planning to go to the media, to expose the family, tell everyone what had happened and what Ted was doing. I begged her not to. I told her just to quit teaching, to stay out of it. But she wouldn't. If the truth came out, Stephanie would've left Cason Glen. She cared too much what everyone thought, and if her image of a perfect life was shattered, it would send her running.

I couldn't lose her.

I had to fight for her with everything I had, and when Leslie wouldn't listen to reason, I asked her to give me a bit of time to talk to Stephanie and see what I could find out. I reported the gun missing that day and hid it in the woods outside our house. Then, exactly a month later, instead of telling her I wanted a divorce, instead of giving her the chance to send Stephanie running and effectively ruin my life, I ended hers.

The weight of what I'd done had been crushing, though. I had loved Leslie, even if I'd never felt for her the way I did about Stephanie. She was a good wife and she didn't deserve what I'd done to her. So, when I'd been planning to confess to the crime, both dreading the punishment and looking forward to the relief that would come with it, Stephanie had given me a way out. She'd saved the day.

When she'd told Jude it had been Ted, I saw, with perfect clarity, how easily everything else would fall into place. When questioned, Principal Warner and the students would be able to back up the story with the truth about Leslie's campaign to out Ted for his...*extracurriculars.* With Ted gone, there was no one to defend him or contradict the lie.

It had all fallen into place, but for what?

If Stephanie didn't trust me now, what was the point of it all?

I'd given up everything for her. Risked everything. And now, I was going to lose her anyway.

CHAPTER THIRTY

STEPHANIE

Two weeks later, the confirmation came in. My husband's dental records were a match for the adult male body they'd found at the bottom of Lake Guinevere. He was dead.

Ted was gone.

I was officially, legally, a widow.

There was no true relief in the realization. Instead, I felt grief. I felt the weight of his loss, the pain of knowing I'd celebrated his disappearance. I'd believed he ran away with someone else, that he'd given up on us as I had, and that he was happier without me. I didn't spend a day grieving our relationship because I'd stopped loving or caring about him the moment I found him in bed with a student. He was dead to me then.

But now, he was just dead.

Truth be told, I should've given up on him sooner than I did. I'd long suspected he was having affairs, but to admit it would mean bringing shame to our family. Especially to me. People would say *well of course he had to find someone else.*

They'd blame me. I'd go back to being invisible. Or worse, despised. I couldn't do that. Instead, I had to play the oblivious wife. I had to pretend everything was fine. I had to keep up whatever image I had left. In such a small town, people talk. If anything were to cause a rift between Ted and me, I would be the one the public turned against.

I'd seen it over and over again in school. Anyone on the outs with Ted, was on the outs with everyone. He made the rules. He set the tone. I couldn't have him turning everyone against me, certainly not my sons.

No, it was worth it to suffer through. It wasn't a great life, but I had a job I loved, boys I'd move heaven and earth for, and the rest would be just fine.

Except, now, he was gone and nothing was fine.

With Ted gone, dead for months according to Jude, that left no suspects in Sophie's murder. And, of course, there was still the question of who'd killed my husband in the first place.

I'd run through my list of suspects, but I kept going back to Enzo. It was the only thing that made sense. If he'd killed Leslie, too, if I'd been wrong about that being Ted, it could've meant that Enzo took out both our spouses for the chance to be with me.

I'd traded one monster for another.

Did I believe he was capable of such things? No, maybe not, but then again, I'd never believed Ted was either.

People surprise you in the worst ways and, at the end of the day, we're all capable of doing monstrous things if it means protecting the people or things we care about most.

A few hours after the call about Ted's body came, I received another. Jude wanted to talk to the boys down at the station. Because they were still minors for another few months, he wanted me to give permission. And, of course, withholding permission would only make me look as if I believed they had something to hide.

The only problem was, I didn't know that they *didn't*.

After all, it was Dom who'd been with Sophie in the driveway. Dom, who'd gone to pick her up. Dom, who seemed the closest to her, despite both of their insistences to the contrary. But why would he want to kill her?

The answer, the thing to click into place and make it all make sense, just wasn't there.

I tried to replay the day of the social in my mind. Rafael had been in his room, but Dom was there with his friends. Had he stayed in my sight the whole time?

No.

I'd lost track of him multiple times. He'd been with his friends. He'd been in and out of their houses. When I'd come inside, he'd been gone for hours. He had the perfect amount of time to do whatever Jude was ready to accuse him of.

It was ridiculous to even contemplate, but I knew who my boys were emulating. I'd watched them change, following in their dad's footsteps, laughing when he spoke about women in a way that made me cringe. High-fiving him when they were taking out one of the popular girls, talking in secret about their love lives.

I couldn't put anything past any of them, and that was the irrefutable truth.

As much as I loved them, I couldn't say they were innocent. And, if I couldn't, who would?

There was only one thing I could do, and it would make me as much of a monster as the rest of them if I was wrong.

I made my way down the hall and toward Dom's bedroom. I knocked carefully, waiting.

"Dom?" I called, when he hadn't answered.

He laughed but didn't respond.

I twisted the handle, but it was locked. "Dom?" I called louder, pounding on the door.

"Hang on," I heard him say. And then to me, "Yeah?"

"What are you doing in there? Let me in."

I heard the bed groan, then his heavy footsteps dragging across the floor. When he pulled it open, his hair was disheveled, his headphones around his neck. "What?"

"I need to talk to you." I wrung my hands together in front of me.

"Can it wait? I'm playing a game."

"No," I said. "It can't wait."

He groaned, rolling his eyes, and pulled his headphones back on. "Hey, bro, I gotta go. Mom's being a total B."

I let the comment go, too much else on my mind. When he took the headphones off and turned them off, along with the TV, I stood in the center of his room, looking around at the mess. Everywhere I looked, there were discarded plates, dirty clothes, and rotting food.

I looked away. None of that mattered right then. "I need to ask you about the day of the social. The day Sophie died."

He kicked back on his bed, his hands under his neck casually. "Mmkay."

"Did you leave the neighborhood that day? After I'd gone inside?"

His expression changed, but only slightly. I saw the flicker of worry. "No, why?"

"Are you lying to me?"

"Why would I be?"

"Did you go down to the lake with Sophie?"

He tensed and, for the first time, looked my way. "Why would you ask that?"

"Because the police want to talk to you and your brother about that day, and I need to know the truth before they find out." I scanned the room carefully, my eyes landing on a small, tan camisole sticking out from under the edge of his dresser. I crossed the room, scooping it up in my hands. "What is this?"

His eyes widened and he sat up straight, tucking one leg under himself. "I don't know."

"Why is it in your room?"

"I have no idea what it is."

"You're lying to me."

"No, I'm—"

"This is Sophie's, Dominic. This is Sophie's camisole. Why is it in your room?"

He swallowed, standing up. "I-I have no idea. It's probably yours."

"It's not mine! You're lying to me! You were with her, weren't you? Did you hurt her, Dom? Did you kill Sophie?"

"Mom!" he cried, his eyes filling with sudden, angry tears. "How can you ask me that?"

"What am I supposed to think? Why else would you have some of her clothing here?"

"Because she stayed the night!" he screamed, covering his eyes.

We stood in silence for a moment. "She what?"

"After she had me pick her up, she stayed here for a few nights until she could talk her uncle into letting her stay there."

"You had a girl staying here without my knowledge?"

"I've already told you, we weren't together like that. You saw us that day, but I haven't even kissed her other than that. She's like...obsessed with some dude who won't text her back."

"Did that make you mad?"

He laughed then, through his tears. "What are you talking about? I could care less. I've got plenty of options."

"Were you with her the day she died? At the lake?"

"Mom, I don't want to talk about it—"

"Well, you'd damn sure better start talking, because it's either me or the police. They want to talk to you both down at the station, and I need to know what they're going to find out."

"Raf only went because I asked him to go. He had nothing to do with any of this!"

"Oh, how noble, that you'd cover for the brother who was supposed to be grounded." I was crying then, my body trembling with white-hot rage. I wadded the camisole in my fist. "What have you done, Dom? Why did you do this?"

"I didn't," he cried, covering his eyes. "I'm sorry, Mom. I swear to you, I didn't do anything. I'm innocent, you have to believe me."

"Why would you even go down there? Why would you meet her at the lake if you had nothing to do with this?" I tried to simmer down my rage with facts. I wanted to believe him. When I looked at my son, I still saw the chubby-faced toddler who'd bring me flowers from the yard and share his Play-Doh ice cream with me, but that wasn't who he was anymore. That wasn't who either of my children were. "I don't know. She asked me to meet her. I thought we were just going to hang. She was supposed to be bringing a friend."

"And what happened when you got there? Why didn't you tell me any of this? I could've protected you. We could've told Jude about all of this from the beginning. Telling him the truth now will only make you look like you were trying to hide it."

His eyes began to water with sudden, fresh tears. "Are we going to go to jail?"

"I don't know," I told him honestly. "Should you? What happened when you got to the lake?"

"We didn't kill her, Mom. I swear we didn't."

"Then what happened?" I demanded.

"She was… She was already there when we got there. She was dead. We thought she was just lying on the sand, but she was sort of…twisted up. I don't know. When we realized she was dead, we just ran. I didn't know what else to do." He fell into my arms without warning, his body shaking with sobs.

I was still for a moment before my arms went around him, my hands rubbing soothing circles in his hair and down his back. "I'm so sorry. I'm so sorry," he whispered into my chest.

"Shhhh," I tried to calm him. "Everything's going to be okay. I'm going to fix this."

He leaned back, wiping his eyes. "How can you?"

"I don't know, but I will. I promise. I'll figure something out."

He hugged me tight. "I love you, Mom. I'm so sorry."

"Just don't ever mention this again. Either of you. Don't tell anyone what you've told me. I'll get rid of this and fix everything." I walked out of his room, camisole still in my hand, fresh tears in my eyes. How could I have been so blind? All this time. All this time I'd allowed myself to be lied to by men over and over again, and now I was having to clean up their messes. But what choice did I have?

My sons may not be the young, flower-picking, Play-Doh sharing boys they once were, but I was still their mother. It was still my job to protect them from everything I could.

I pulled my phone out of my pocket and dialed Jude's number, my hands shaking. I hated myself for it before it was done.

"Hello?"

"Jude, I was wrong."

"Stephanie?" He sounded like he was outside, the wind blowing into his speaker and making him hard to hear.

"I was wrong. It wasn't Ted," I said, speaking louder.

"What wasn't Ted?"

"Sophie—"

"Well, yeah, we worked that out with the timeline."

"He didn't kill Leslie either."

"What? Are you sure? How do you know?"

"I'm sure. It was Enzo," I said plainly, covering my mouth in between silent sobs. "He just confessed to me. He killed them both."

CHAPTER THIRTY-ONE

MICHELLE

Jude hadn't been home in more than a day and, when he'd actually answered my calls, he'd been short and to the point. He hadn't given me an update on what was going on or told me what I should be expecting. Were we going to be arrested? I knew they'd confirmed that the body was Ted's, but since then…nothing.

So, with my hair curled, one of my favorite dresses on, and a lunch box packed with his favorite meal, I headed into town toward my husband's station with outright fear bubbling in my stomach.

It felt weird, to be so on edge. It was how I remembered feeling the day after everything happened. The waiting and wondering of when we were going to be found out.

This was different, as there was no more wondering. Just waiting.

I pulled up to the station and climbed out of the car, walking up the stairs and past Millie.

"Hey, Mrs. Rivera," she said, waving at me casually. Had she stared at me for an extra moment? Had she said hello the way she'd greet a suspect? I couldn't tell.

"Is Jude in his office?" I pointed toward the closed door.

"Been here all night."

"Thank you." I approached the door, knocking carefully before pushing it open. He was behind the desk, hastily scribbling something down on one of the papers in front of him. When he looked up, he seemed confused.

"What are you doing here?" he asked, standing to greet me.

"I brought you some lunch. Thought you might be hungry."

He glanced at the large, round clock on the wall, then ran a hand over his forehead, blowing out a puff of air. "Is it three o'clock already?"

I nodded, shutting the door behind me and placing the lunch bag on the only clear space on his desk. "You didn't call me last night."

"I was planning to come home before you woke up. I've just been"—he gestured toward the desk—"knee deep in all of this."

"Well, you still need to eat." I began unzipping the bag.

"Aren't you going to ask me for an update?"

"I've learned you'll give me one when you're ready."

He stared at me, reading through the lie. If the case didn't affect me, I would've been digging into everything he could tell me, but with this, I was in no real hurry to know. Not when the only outcome would be bad news.

To my surprise, he placed his hands on top of mine, stopping me from laying out the food. "We have a suspect."

"A—what? What do you mean?"

He lowered his voice, sinking down into his chair, and I followed his lead, sitting down across from him. "Enzo has confessed to killing Leslie, Ted, and Sophie."

I jerked my head back, shaking it simultaneously. "No, he didn't. He…" I checked to make sure his door was still shut before saying in a hushed whisper, "Ted, he couldn't have."

"But he did."

"Why would he do that?" I furrowed my brow. Had Jude done something? Held something over his friend's head? "We know Enzo. He wouldn't have killed anyone…"

He raised one shoulder in a shrug. "He knows us too, and I'm sure he's thinking the same thing."

"Well, we didn't *kill* anyone. Besides, you know it's not true, Jude. You can't seriously be thinking of arresting him."

His voice was near a whisper. "We know he didn't kill Ted, yes. But we don't know that he didn't kill Leslie and Sophie. And, if he did, he's going to jail anyway. Isn't it better that he goes than…anyone else?" He leaned forward. "I mean, we didn't *do* anything, really, you're right. That's kind of the brilliance of all this. Who would you rather see go—Enzo or Caroline?"

"Neither."

"Well, someone has to answer for this. I can't sweep three murders under the rug, and that's not even mentioning the three other bodies we found that I still have to try and iden-tify. So, if Enzo doesn't get arrested, it puts Caroline at risk of being found out. You know how quickly news travels here, if even one person knows about her and Ted—"

"You know I'd take the blame in a heartbeat over her."

"I do. And so would I. But where does that leave Caroline, if we go away? And the baby? She needs us. *They* need us."

I shook my head. "I don't…I can't…" I suddenly couldn't catch my breath. He shot up from his desk, taking my hands and placing them on his cheeks.

"Breathe," he instructed. "Just breathe."

I did as I was told, focusing on his eyes as I drew out a long inhale, then exhaled. "I just, I mean, Jude, this is Enzo we're talking about."

"And Ted was Ted," he said firmly. "All that matters to me right now is protecting you and Caroline. Above all else."

"Do you really think he killed Leslie?" Ted had always slept around, even when we were in school, so while it shocked me that he was sleeping with our daughter, it hadn't been entirely out of character for him. This, though, that our closest friend, the Enzo I'd only ever seen be comforting and loving, could've committed not one, but two murders... How much of my world would have to be torn apart before I realized that nothing was what I believed? Everyone had secrets, I couldn't trust even those I considered my closest friends, and we had to protect ourselves.

Jude was right, but that didn't make it any less hard.

I noticed then, the red splotches under his eyes, the bloodshot quality that I thought meant he was only tired.

But now I understood the truth. He'd been crying, too.

I realized then why he'd stayed at the office all night. Not because he'd been busy, but because he'd been dealing with his own moral dilemma in the only way he knew how. He wanted to hide the panic from me, to keep me from second-guessing a decision he'd already made.

We'd buried one friend, and now we'd ruin another. All for our child. It was an impossible decision, and yet there was no decision to be made. It was the only choice there was.

He lowered his lips to mine gently, then brushed away a tear I hadn't felt on my cheek.

"We have to do this. Not for us, but for Caroline. For our family."

It was as simple and as complicated as that.

We'd already crossed one line, betrayed one friend, so what was one more in the scope of things? Especially if Enzo really had done what Jude was accusing him of. He was right. Besides Ted, we didn't know the truth of what had happened to Leslie and Sophie. Wasn't it better to believe their killer was put away than to worry that we had a serial killer loose in Cason Glen?

"Have you talked to him?"

He shook his head. "I'm bringing him in for questioning tomorrow."

"Do you have enough to prove he did it?"

"Enough to arrest him, yes. His alibi falls flat when presented with the new evidence. It would've been easy enough to have someone else give him that receipt or to even fake a receipt. The payment was in cash, so there's really no trail. No surveillance tape, toll roads, traffic cams. A confession to Stephanie, the murder weapon, the bodies. Motive."

"Motive?"

"Stephanie said he told her he killed Ted and Leslie to be with her. Their relationship has been going on much longer than either of us realized, and he got tired of waiting for her to leave him."

"And Sophie?"

"Sophie found out the truth about what he'd done to her aunt and was planning to tell. He killed her to protect his secret."

I sucked in a sharp breath. It was too hard to imagine. Even harder to believe. Leslie had been my friend. She was a good person, a good teacher, an excellent neighbor. She didn't deserve to die, but especially not at the hand of the man she'd loved more than life. And poor Sophie, with so much life ahead of her. I couldn't help thinking of Caroline, comparing the two. They were so young. They had so much life left. What would I do if someone had hurt her? Or tried to?

I knew the answer, because the last person who'd tried just had his bones discovered in Lake Guinevere. If all of this was true, Enzo deserved to go to prison as much as Ted deserved to die. How was it I'd managed to find one of the only good men left in Cason Glen? I reached forward, filled with admiration for my husband, and laced my fingers through his. He kissed my wrist, looking troubled even as he made the warm gesture.

"Why would Stephanie turn him in, though, if they were together? Why would he confess it to her in the first place?" I asked as the questions occurred to me.

"I don't know," he said simply. "I'm assuming he thought she'd keep his secret, understand why he did it, and she had more loyalty to Ted than he realized."

"Even if he committed the other crimes, I don't understand why he'd confess to something we know he didn't do."

"I don't either, but I can't dwell on it. This is what we've been waiting for... If Enzo goes down, we're finally free. And after what he did to Leslie and Sophie, I can't let myself feel bad about it. Neither should you." His computer chimed, and he glanced over at it then looked at me, remorse in his unsettled expression. "I hate to cut this short, but I really need to get back to work. Thank you for bringing me lunch. I'll be home for dinner, okay?"

"Sure." I nodded, feeling lightheaded after all I'd learned. I stood, patting the lunch box. "Well," I said breathlessly, "I'll get going, then. I'll...I'll see you at home. I love you."

"I love you, too," he called after me.

With that, I walked away, hoping Millie wouldn't notice my silent tears as I passed her on my way out of the building. I couldn't help wondering why my husband was handling this decision so much better than I was.

How had he seemed so calm?

How did he plan to live with himself and the decision we'd made?

Those questions had me mulling over new worse questions: What if I was wrong before? What if my husband wasn't so good after all? What if he was as much a monster as Ted and Enzo were?

What if we were all monsters deep down, after all?

CHAPTER THIRTY-TWO

ENZO

I saw the squad car pull into the drive, lights on, before I heard the knock on the door. Izzy was asleep on the couch, her first good sleep in days, and Darren was sitting at the island, his head in his hands over the mug of coffee I was sure was cold by then.

I'd reminded him about it once, but he didn't care. They couldn't bring themselves to care about anything, and I couldn't blame them. They were broken down, deteriorating with each passing day, and I knew their pain would likely never fully ease.

I felt so useless to them. They needed me to take care of them, to fix this somehow. Just like they'd trusted me to take care of Sophie. I felt such shame at knowing I'd failed them in every way.

As the knocking continued, I made my way out of the kitchen and down the hall, swinging open the door. Jude was there, dressed in uniform, his eyes puffy. He looked near death, pale and downtrodden, and I knew he'd be delivering bad news. Had they found something out about Sophie?

"Hey man, what's up?"

He cleared his throat, staring directly into my eyes as he reached for his cuffs. Time seemed to slow down as I heard him begin to speak.

"Lorenzo Barone, you're under arrest for the murders of Leslie Barone, Theodore Dupont, and Sophia Green..." His words became fuzzy as he instructed me to turn around and put my hands behind my back.

For just a moment, I was sure it was a joke. I knew he had to be kidding, but there was nothing in his eyes that told me so.

"What are you talking about?" I scoffed.

The noise had woken Izzy, and she and Darren were walking toward us, down a hallway that suddenly seemed much longer than usual, their haunted eyes full of disbelief.

"What's going on, Jude?" Izzy asked.

He shook his head, nudging my shoulder so I began to turn. "Go back inside, Izzy."

"Let go of me, man," I jerked out of his grasp. "You have to tell me what's going on."

"Don't make this harder than it has to be," he said, slamming the first cuff onto my wrist without warning.

"What's happening?" Izzy wailed, fresh tears in the eyes I'd been sure couldn't produce any more.

"Go back inside, sis. I'll be okay." I began to cooperate, if only to keep her calm. I let him put the other cuff on me without fuss. "Everything's fine. Just a misunderstanding." Jude led me to his car without another word. It was the first time I'd ridden in the back of it.

Even as he ushered me into the seat and hurried around to the driver's door, I expected him to look back, crack a smile, and say this was all a joke.

Instead, he climbed inside, not saying a word as we pulled out of my drive, around the grassy circle I'd danced on just days earlier, past Stephanie's house, and out of the subdivision.

It wasn't until we reached the station that I realized this was really real. Really happening.

And I had no idea why.

He let me out of the car and led me into the room I'd been in just days before, removing my handcuffs and sitting down across from me. There was a tape recorder in the center of the table this time, and he pressed a button. I immediately heard the whirring of the tapes turning inside.

"Everything you say in this room will be on official record. I need you to speak slowly and clearly."

"Are you going to tell me what's going on now?"

"Can you please state your name for the record?"

"You know my name."

"I need you to say it."

"Enz—Lorenzo Malakai Barone."

"Mr. Barone, you have the right to a lawyer. Do you have one? If not, I will have one brought in for you. They will be independent of the police, and their services will be provided for free."

"I don't need a lawyer, man. Just fuckin' talk to me."

"You're officially waiving your rights to counsel, then? For the record." He pointed to the tape recorder, as if I could forget it was there.

"Yeah, whatever. I'm waiving *yada yada*."

"Okay, then. I spared the details for your sister's sake," he told me, folding his hands in front of him.

"What the hell are you even talking about? You know I had nothing to do with Sophie's death. Or Ted's, for God's sake. And Stephanie told you about Leslie—"

"Stephanie has since recanted her original statement."

The words were a gut punch. "Sh-she *what?*"

"We have a sworn statement from Stephanie that you confessed to all three murders."

"I—" I stared into space; nothing about what he was saying made any sense. I thought back to the last conversation with Stephanie, the fight in her bedroom when she'd accused me of killing Leslie and Ted. But I hadn't killed Ted. I definitely hadn't. And I certainly hadn't confessed to killing anyone. "I didn't... I don't understand why she would tell you that. Let me talk to her."

"It's not possible, Enzo. Not right now."

"Is this all a joke? Is this a literal prank right now?"

"I wouldn't joke like this. It's time to start telling me the truth. About everything."

"The truth?" I slammed my fist on the table. "The truth is I have no idea what's going on. I never confessed to killing anyone to Stephanie. I don't know why she'd do this. We had a fight—"

"You think she'd craft up this story over a fight?" He stared at me skeptically.

"No, but what else am I supposed to think? You have to believe me, man." I pounded my hands against my chest. "It's me. You know me. You know I'd never do this."

"I'm afraid it's not up to me, Enzo. We have her statement, and she has no reason to lie. We have motive, we have the weapon. Even if I wanted to, I couldn't help you."

"Motive? For killing my niece? My best friend?"

"For killing the husband of the woman you were having an affair with," he said, then pursed his lips. "She told us about that, too. It had been going on for years."

"Yeah, but..." I blinked, trying to think, to put it all together. Why had she done this? Why would she want to ruin me? "I had no reason to kill Sophie. She was... God, man, I loved her. She drove me crazy some days, but she meant so much to me. I'd never do that to her, or to Izzy. Sophie was the closest thing I had to a daughter."

Tears lined my eyes, spilling over onto my cheeks. "Please don't do this. Izzy will never recover if she thinks I had anything to do with Sophie's death. You have to believe me about this."

"Then you need to start talking."

"I've said all I have to say. Stephanie's lying, period."

"Why would she be lying?"

"*I have no idea*," I bellowed smartly, smacking the table again. "If you'd let me out of here, I'd ask her. Or better yet, why don't you go do your job and find out? Maybe *she* killed them."

He turned his head to the side slightly, as if I was testing him. "I've done my job, and the evidence points to you, Enzo. We have means, motive, and opportunity. Plus Stephanie's statement. From here, it's really out of my hands."

"What do you mean it's out of your hands? You're the sheriff. I'm your best friend. You have to fix this! You can fix this, I know you can, so do it. I'm telling you the truth. Come on, Jude, you can't seriously be going to let me go to jail for this. We're like brothers, man."

Jude stood without warning and made his way toward the door. "I've told you there's nothing I can do. So, if there's nothing else you need to tell me, I have to get back to work. Officer Parker will be in to book you. He'll take your belongings, search you for any weapons, then have you finger-printed and photographed. After that, you'll be allowed food and water if you'd like. Any questions?" He pulled the door open.

My heart lurched at the idea of him leaving, of my friend, the person I trusted walking away and leaving me alone. I was going to be arrested. I was going to go to prison.

Well, if I was going to go down, I wanted it to be for the crime I'd actually committed.

I stood up. "I want to confess."

Jude stopped, shutting the door again and making his way back to the table. "Are you sure you don't want to speak to an attorney first?" He checked to be sure the tapes were still recording.

"No," I said, sitting down and picking at a piece of dried skin on my palm. "I just want to tell you."

He took a seat again. "Okay, then. Go on."

I took a deep breath, knowing what I was about to do was completely insane, and began anyway. "I killed my wife." *Breathe.* "I killed Leslie Barone. I shot her using the gun that was found in the lake." Jude swallowed but didn't say anything. "We'd fought, and it was in the heat of the moment. I acted without thinking."

"What were you fighting about?"

"My relationship with Stephanie Dupont. My wife believed Ted Dupont was having an affair with a student, and she wanted to tell. I thought it would cause Stephanie to leave town, and..." *Breathe. Keep it together.* "I love her. I was scared I was going to lose her."

He nodded. "You said you used the gun in the heat of the moment, but a few months earlier, you'd reported that gun missing."

Fuck.

"Yeah, I guess you are good at your job. Okay, I'll admit, that part was a lie. I'd been thinking about it for a while. It was stupid. I loved her. I don't know why I did it." I started crying then, real tears, sobs tearing through me. "I thought about it and how I would do it, and it was our only gun that wasn't registered to me. I didn't want to have one of my guns missing." Even as I said the thoughts aloud, I regretted them.

I hated myself for even coming up with them. What was wrong with me? Why had I done this? What had I done?

"So, you planned to kill her?"

"Not exactly, like not the day and time and stuff, but I set it up so I could when I was ready. And, well, eventually I was ready."

Jude stared at me, his eyes dead and emotionless. "And after you killed her, you dropped the gun into the river?"

"Yeah, I drove over the bridge and threw it out."

"And how did you get the receipt for your alibi? From a bar in Paducah?"

"I had a city employee who was going on a business call that night. Spencer Cavannah. He expensed the meal and had to turn in his receipt."

"So, you did plan it, then? You knew you could do it that night because you'd be getting his receipt?"

Fuck again.

"Yes," I said bitterly, looking down. Then, I looked back up. "Fine. Yeah. It was a horrible mistake. I regret doing it." I held up a finger, as if I could redeem myself. "But I didn't kill Ted or Sophie. I swear to you I didn't."

"Then why did you tell Stephanie that you did?"

"I didn't tell Stephanie anything at all. About Leslie or anything else. I wanna marry that girl, man. Why would I tell her something like this?"

"What cause would she have to lie?"

I squeezed my hands into fists, thinking maybe I'd killed the wrong woman after all. Maybe Leslie was right about everything. Maybe Stephanie was as snakelike as she'd said. Maybe she was covering for Ted all along. "I have no idea."

He nodded. "Is there anything else you want to tell me?"

"That's it," I said, my throat raw. Surprisingly enough, I felt as if a giant weight had been lifted off my shoulders. Whatever happened now, at least I'd spoken my truth. But, as

Jude's unforgiving eyes drilled into mine, I wasn't sure any of that would matter.

I was going down for it all, wasn't I? Somewhere, heaven, whatever, wherever she was, I pictured Leslie laughing.

"No one's invincible." Those were her last words to me, though they'd been about Ted at the time, a rebuttal to my argument that Ted could get away with everything.

As it turns out, she was right. No one was invincible. Least of all, me.

The sound of her laughter in my head grew louder.

CHAPTER THIRTY-THREE

STEPHANIE

I hated myself the moment the call ended. The moment I'd betrayed the final shred of my morality. I'd watched it all fall away, step by step, piece by piece.

I'd lost the first piece when I'd ignored Ted's affairs. Next, when I started an affair of my own. After that, the pieces fell quicker: when I'd found the student in our bed, when I'd heard his thoughts about Leslie and kept my mouth shut, when I'd lied to Enzo over and over about how we'd be together someday before finally telling him it would never happen, when I watched my boys talk about women in ways that disgusted me, when I felt relief not sadness over the fact that Ted had disappeared, when I watched the school honor Ted without getting the courage to tell them what a monster he was, when I told Enzo we could announce our relationship after I knew I was no longer in love with him, and finally, the final piece, the moment I knew I had to lie in order to save my boys.

That was what mothers were supposed to do, wasn't it? Wasn't I supposed to protect them, even when I knew they'd done something terrible?

Should I have turned them in instead? Should I have let them go to prison for what they'd done? Maybe, but would you?

Would you turn your own child in? Ask yourself that before you judge me.

Because maybe a better mother would've. Maybe a better mother would've told the truth to save them from themselves, to save someone else from their destruction, but I couldn't do it.

I'd die to protect them, and I had to believe they deserved it. They were just children, after all. Still just boys at the end of the day. They needed me. They needed me more than ever with Ted gone, and I'd been away. I'd been working two demanding jobs, leaving them to deal with their grief, to process something so unspeakable, all on their own.

They were ill-equipped, and I'd failed them. I'd failed them in so many ways—by staying with their father when I knew he was a bad influence, by not speaking up more often, and by disappearing when they needed me most.

Now, though, now that I knew everything, I could fix them. I could get them into therapy. Force them. Drag them kicking and screaming if I had to. I could make them see the error of their ways, make them see the consequences that could've been theirs, and I could force them to straighten up.

It was the least I could do for them after failing them so badly.

So, the next morning, I met the boys in the kitchen, cornering them before they'd had a chance to bolt. I wanted them to understand what I'd done for them.

"Boys, I need to talk to you both."

"Seriously?" Raf asked, taking a drink from the mug of coffee in his hand.

"It's not even nine a.m. How could we already be in trouble?" Dom asked.

"I wanted you to know that Enzo Barone has been arrested for your father's murder. And Sophie's."

They were solemn. Neither of them had said much since I told them their father was no longer missing, but dead. Instead, they'd spent most of the time since the announcement in their rooms, playing games with their friends and avoiding me. I wasn't sure what the healthiest ways to cope with grief were, I certainly wasn't handling it the right way either, but I knew they needed help that I could no longer give them.

"Cool," Dom said finally, pulling an energy drink from the refrigerator.

"And, um—" I was caught off guard by the cavalier response, but I went on. "I think you should both start seeing a therapist. We all should. We're going to. To help us process everything that's happened."

"No way," Raf said.

"Eff that," Dom sneered.

"I know you probably don't want to because you're worried about what people will think, but you don't have to. We don't have to tell anyone who we're seeing or what we're doing. No one will know there's anything going on. And, even if they were to find out, there's no shame in seeing someone, but I promise you they won't. It'll just be between us."

"Between you and you, maybe. We aren't going," Dom said, belching loudly. "Did you not hear us?"

"Dom, don't be like this. After everything we talked about yesterday—"

"What'd you talk about yesterday?" Raf asked, the question directed to his brother, not me.

Dom smirked. "Mom knows about..." He paused, moving his hand to the front of his face and making an exploding motion with his fingers, complete with sound effects, as if to replicate the fatal blow to Sophie's head.

Raf turned to look at me, his eyes icy. "How does she know?"

"It doesn't matter how," I told him, trying to keep my wits about me. My son had never scared me, but in that moment, as he towered over me, his dark eyes lifeless and cold, I felt scared for my life. I brushed the worry away. It was ridiculous. "The important thing is that I'd never tell anyone. And now that Enzo's been arrested, you don't have to worry about anything. I-I took care of it."

His shoulders dropped their tension, and he took another drink of his coffee. "You did that for us?"

"I'd do anything for you boys, you know that."

He seemed to contemplate the statement for a moment before saying, "Good to know."

"But I'm sure you both have feelings about what happened, and you need a safe space to process them."

He shrugged, his bottom lip puckered out in a way that said *feelings, what are those?* "I don't have any feelings I need to process. What about you, Dom?"

"Nope, no feelings here," his brother teased.

My blood ran cold. How could they act so unfazed by what had happened? I wasn't even there, I was entirely innocent, and I still found myself crying over what had happened. I felt terrible for Sophie, for Izzy, for our community. I knew they wanted to seem tough, but they had to feel some of that, too. How could they not? "Surely that's not true. You were... intimate with the girl, Dom. You must care about her."

"*Intimate?*" Raf chuckled, slapping his brother's chest. "What is this? The eighteen hundreds? Jesus, Mom. They just fucked. They weren't married."

Dom chuckled as I flinched. "I've told you I don't like that language."

He lowered his face toward me, spittle forming in the corner of his mouth. *"Fuck, fuck, fuckety, fuck."*

I glowered at him. "Rafael! You are still a child. You're still *my* child. You have to listen to me. Don't you understand what I've done for you? What I've sacrificed to do it?"

"What you've sacrificed?" he asked with a doubtful scowl. "What? You mean Enzo? Come on, Mom, that dude was the worst."

"That *dude* just went to jail for a crime you committed, Raf. Maybe show him a little respect."

He looked at Dom, a strange expression on his face, then back at me. Finally, one corner of his mouth upturned into a sneer. "No, Mom. I killed a girl. Maybe you should show *me* a little respect."

With that, he stormed past me, Dom following in step, and I heard them laughing down the hall. A cold chill swept through my body, from my toes to my chest, where it swelled with a new form of hopelessness.

I killed a girl.

The words repeated in my head, the threat of his statement. I knew what they'd done, but somehow, hearing it said aloud, said in that way, it felt different. Worse.

They didn't feel regret or remorse over what they'd done. They were bragging about it. Laughing about it.

It was obvious my boys were beyond saving, but where did that leave me? I didn't want to give up on them, but how could I live with myself if I continued to overlook their behavior? It would be no better than what I'd done with Ted. I needed to act now, to stop the cycle before they ended up just like their father in every way.

I ran through my options, shivering in the kitchen as I kept replaying the steely, wicked way he'd been staring at me.

I hated it. I hated feeling this way. It was as if the blindfold had finally been removed and I could see them for what they were. No longer misunderstood, they were monsters. Plain and simple, and no amount of time would allow that weight to feel any better in my heart.

I loved them, despite it all, but I had to make a decision. I could save the world from my boys, or I could continue trying to fix them, continue trying to break through.

Even knowing what I knew, finally accepting what I had, believing that my boys were every bit as bad as their father, the decision I made next was the hardest decision I have ever or will ever make in my life.

CHAPTER THIRTY-FOUR

CAROLINE

TWO MONTHS LATER

The pain was excruciating. Red-hot fire coursing through my body. I screamed, crying out for someone, anyone to make it stop. *Please.*

"I'm dying!" I screamed. Mom was at my side, holding my hand and stroking my hair.

"Just a bit longer, sweetheart. Keep breathing." She kept kissing my forehead, her tears dripping onto my face as she whispered to me what a good job I was doing.

Good job or not, I wanted it over.

It hurts. They warn you that it hurts, but they don't warn you that—

Oh my god, it hurts like I'm being ripped apart in every direction. Someone's lit me on fire. I'm being electrocuted. Burned at the stake. This is what the witches went through. This is the literal worst. Jesus fuc—

"One more big push," the doctor between my legs was saying. I squeezed every one of my muscles, pushing and screaming as if my life depended on it. I was going to get this baby out, or I was going to die. There were no more options. I couldn't handle another second of the pain. Not one more—

"Waaaah!"

Cries.

Tiny, electric, angry.

I heard the wails in an instant. It was a sound I'd only heard on television shows or whenever I'd visit my friends' houses and they had newborn siblings there.

The pain dulled almost instantly, and suddenly there was a squirming, purple and bloody infant hanging above me. They plopped her—"It's a girl," I heard Mom cry out—down onto my stomach still covered in goop straight out of a horror film, and her cries calmed almost immediately.

"Put your arms around her," Mom instructed, lifting my hands to my stomach so I could hold my baby.

Our baby.

The baby that was supposed to be ours. I held her then, snapping out of my stupor. I stared at her little features, trying to pick out which came from me and which came from her father.

"You're so beautiful," I told her in a whisper. The room had grown silent, at least as far as I could tell. At that moment, she and I were the only things that existed.

But, all too soon, they were taking her from me and placing her under a light. Poking and prodding her, weighing and measuring. Numbers and figures were called out, most making no sense to me, and I watched her like a hawk.

Bring her back, I wanted to cry. *She's mine.*

Mom eased down on the bed next to me, brushing my hair out of my face. I was sweaty and gross, and there was still a doctor between my legs. "She's beautiful, sweetheart. You did so well."

She was crying, and I realized then, I was too. Mom dried

my tears gently, her own eyes glistening. "I'm so proud of you."

"We'll call her Carrie," I said. The nickname Ted had given me. I remembered him whispering it in my ear so many times.

You're so beautiful, Carrie.

I've missed you, Carrie.

I like it when you wear your hair like that, Carrie.

I'm never going to leave you, Carrie.

It's different with you, Carrie.

It would be the way I chose to honor his memory. His final gift to me and my final gift to him.

"Carrie?" Mom mulled it over. "After you? I love it." She smiled because she didn't know the truth behind the name, and she never would.

When they brought her back to me, I stared down at the baby, somehow even more beautiful than before. I kissed her head, breathing in her scent.

I'd do anything for you, I told her silently, and with a blink of her tired eyes, I knew she understood. It was just her and me. Forever.

As the doctors finished up and began filing out of the room, Mom stood from the bed, wiping her tears. "I'm going to go get your father," she whispered, kissing my head. I nodded, but I wasn't really listening. I was only focused on my daughter.

"Your daddy would've loved you," I told her, kissing her forehead again. Someday, I knew she'd ask about her father, and though I didn't have to worry about that for quite some time, I couldn't help thinking about what I'd tell her.

That he'd loved her but we couldn't be together. That I'd loved her more than our relationship. That I'd chosen her over everyone and that I always, always would.

I'd never tell her the truth. Never tell anyone.

No one could know that Ted had wanted to break up after he found out I was pregnant. That it had all gotten too real for him. The abortion story wasn't a lie, necessarily. He hadn't said it in so many words, but he hadn't wanted to be with me either way. And how was I going to raise his child in the same town as him while keeping his secret?

When I told him I couldn't, I wouldn't, he'd tried to make me see reason. He asked me to pick him up and bring him down to the lake. He said we could talk there, in the middle of the night, like we so often did. It was the only time our sleepy little town allowed us to be together without curious, nosy onlookers.

But when we got there, moving down to the safety and security the bridge provided, I hadn't changed my mind. We'd fought about it for a while. I told him if I couldn't have him, no one would. He was mad, frustrated, mumbling to himself about how difficult I was and why he'd ever chosen me, and he'd turned to walk away. He was leaving me. Planning to, anyway, when I swung the rock. I hadn't even realized it was in my hand until I was already connecting it with his skull.

He stumbled, fell face first into the sand, and I rolled him over without much protest and climbed onto his stomach. I slammed the rock into his face again and again and again. *If I can't have you, no one will.* I repeated it over and over, bringing the rock down on his skull until no one would ever have him again. No one but me. I would forever own his final moment, his last memory.

When it was done, I cleaned myself up before calling my parents, the rest of my plan falling into place.

I didn't want to kill him. Honestly, I didn't. I wanted him to realize his mistake, but it was obvious he wouldn't. And there was no way I was going to go down as the girl who got knocked up in high school while he took none of the blame for starting our entire relationship.

There had been other girls, girls he'd gotten into trouble who'd disappeared. There were rumors. Some said he'd sent them away, given them money to start a new life, but others —darker stories—said he'd killed them. I'd heard talk about it around school. I didn't know the truth about the other girls, but Ted would never have hurt me. He would never lie to me. I was special.

I wasn't stupid enough to think I was the only girl he was sleeping with, but I knew I was the only girl he loved.

I thought our child would be different.

I thought he'd want us both. That was what he'd told me. *Forever.* The pregnancy was supposed to cement our relationship. I was finally almost eighteen, and so were his kids. It was time for him to leave his wife, his family, and build a new one. With me.

But, out of nowhere, he decided that wasn't what he wanted. He wasn't going to choose me after all, so I took any choice he'd ever have away from him.

That was supposed to be the end of it, too, if it weren't for stupid Dominic and Rafael Dupont.

I'd done well to hide my belly behind baggy clothes at school and around town, but one day between classes, Raf had pinned me against a wall in the gym and put his hand between my legs, shoving his tongue in my mouth with an unappealing kiss.

I tried to shove him off, but he was strong, unmoving. I would've barfed if I didn't feel the need to laugh when, in an attempt to feel me up, his hand grazed my belly and he froze. He jumped back, physically repulsed by the brother or sister I'd soon be bringing into the world.

Dumb as they were, together, I guessed they managed to figure out what had happened. They knew about Ted and me. He liked to bring me to their house when Stephanie was at work, bringing me down the hall a few extra times or into the rooms where his sons were to make sure they would see me. He got a special thrill out of it, like he was competing with them. Like I was the prize and he'd won.

But, all that time, they'd kept quiet about our relationship. When he felt my belly, when they figured out I was pregnant, the brothers began tormenting me. They asked about their father, blaming me for his disappearance and threatening to tell.

They thought maybe he'd run off with me, that I knew where he was. Or maybe they thought he'd found out I was pregnant and bolted, I'm not entirely sure.

Either way, I didn't want to kill even once, and certainly not twice, but what choice did I have?

I was going to tell the boys that I'd tell them what happened if they met me at the lake the day of the social, when all the adults were distracted, but first I needed to decide on a plan. I thought about trying to kill them both, but it was too risky. The bigger I got, the clumsier I was, and they were stronger than me, especially together.

So, when I saw Sophie talking to Mom, I saw my chance. I followed her back to her uncle's house and apologized for my mom. Then, I asked if she wanted to get out of there. I told her I knew where Ted was—*genius.*

I knew she had a thing for him. I remembered her hanging around the house so often during the summer she'd stayed with Enzo. Ted never cared about her, not like he did me, but she didn't need to know that. I told her he'd texted me and we were meeting at the beach. Then I asked her to text the brothers. I said Ted wanted it to be a surprise and that she should text Dom and tell him to meet us.

She never mentioned my name, I don't know if she didn't remember it or if she just wanted to take the credit for reuniting them with their father in the end, but it worked out so well for me anyway.

We'd walked to the lake—she didn't have a car there and I couldn't chance my parents seeing me leave, so I insisted I wanted to stretch my legs—and I directed her to the place under the base of the bridge where Ted and I had hidden so many times. I picked up a rock similar to the one I'd used to kill Ted and smacked her over the head with it. She'd died quicker than him, gone down easier, and it was a good thing. I felt no anger toward her, despite the fact that she was in love with the father of my child. She was just a means to an end.

I placed her body carefully so, from a distance, it looked like she was sitting there, waiting for them.

Then, when the boys arrived, I hid in the bushes not far away and snapped several pictures of them with the body. As I expected, they bolted at realizing she was dead, but I sent them the picture straightaway, with a short phone call afterward to let them know our new deal: if they ever told anyone about their father and me, I'd show everyone the pictures. And they couldn't kill me or steal my phone, because I'd already backed up the photo to my cloud, meaning if I disappeared, the police were sure to find it.

They thought they were smart, but I would've paid big money to see the looks on their faces that day. They had no idea what I was capable of. So often, I was underestimated, but I always found a way to prove myself.

And, look, I feel bad about it, okay? Sophie was nice enough, but I had to do it. I had to.

If the boys told anyone, I'd go to prison. I'd lose my daughter.

As I stared down into her eyes, I knew I'd made the right decision. The boys were awaiting trial after their mother turned them in—*their own mother!* It turned out they didn't even need the photos to go down for a crime they didn't commit. Which, honestly, they definitely deserved to be in prison. Even if they weren't murderers, they were absolute lunatics. The worst of the worst. Like every living person on the planet, I'd heard the rumors about all the girls they'd forced themselves on, the naked pictures they'd forwarded around to all the guys in school. They were animals, and I'd done society a favor by making sure they could never hurt anyone else.

I wouldn't regret it. Any of it.

Not for a second.

The door opened, and my parents walked in, their eyes full of love for the life I'd brought into the world. It was almost as if I were settling the score in a way.

I'd ended two lives, but created a new one. *A better one.*

She was innocent.

Beautiful.

Perfect.

The best parts of her father and me, and she'd grow into a woman who could protect herself. A woman who knew what the world was like. I'd protect her with all I had, like I'd already done and like my parents had done for me.

I kissed her head again, breathing in her scent before handing her to my mother, whose arms were outstretched, eyes still full of tears.

My daughter didn't know I'd made the choice to become a monster in order to protect her, and she never would.

At least, not unless she ever needed me to again.

After all, what are parents for if not to protect their children however they can?

The way I see it, we're all part monster. Some of us just hide it better than others.

DON'T MISS THE NEXT
PSYCHOLOGICAL THRILLER FROM
KIERSTEN MODGLIN!

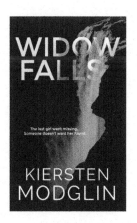

The last girl went missing.
Someone doesn't want her found.

Read *Widow Falls* today:
mybook.to/widowfalls

ENJOYED OUR LITTLE SECRET?

If you enjoyed this story, please consider leaving me a quick review. It doesn't have to be long—just a few words will do. Who knows? Your review might be the thing that encourages a future reader to take a chance on my work!
To leave a review, please visit:
mybook.to/OurLtlScrt

Let everyone know how much you loved
Our Little Secret on Goodreads:
https://bit.ly/OURLTLSCRT

DON'T MISS THE NEXT RELEASE FROM KIERSTEN MODGLIN

Thank you so much for reading this story. I'd love to invite you to sign up for my mailing list and text alerts so we can be sure you don't miss my next release.

Sign up for my mailing list here:
http://eepurl.com/dhiRRv
Sign up for my text alerts here:
www.kierstenmodglinauthor.com/textalerts.html

ACKNOWLEDGMENTS

First and foremost, to my incredible husband and amazing little girl—thank you for always believing in me, cheering me on, and helping me grow. Thank you for all the work you put in to help me reach new readers. For the late nights, the post office runs, the TikTok videos, the ideas, the inspiration, and so much else. I'm forever grateful to be able to do life with the two of you.

To my friend, Emerald O'Brien—this one's for you. I seriously don't know how I ever published without you. You're my closest friend and the person I trust to help me make the big decisions. I'm in awe of your amazing soul, your kindness, your tenacity, and your appreciation for those around you. I couldn't and wouldn't want to do this without you. You're stuck with me!

To my immensely talented editor, Sarah West—I'm so thankful to have you on my team. Over the years, I've grown to rely on you and trust you with every decision and story idea. You've taken my book babies and helped make them shine a thousand times brighter and, for that, I could never say thank you enough.

To the proofreading team at My Brother's Editor—thank you for your humor, your insight, and your amazing eagle eye. I'm insanely grateful to be one of your clients. You go above and beyond to make each of my books so much better and I just can't tell you how much I appreciate you.

To two amazing readers—Stephanie Dupont and Michelle Rivera—who won a chance to be featured as characters in this story. I hope you enjoyed meeting and reading about your namesakes.

To my loyal readers (AKA the #KMod Squad)—thank you for being you. Thank you for loving my stories for what they are. For cheering me on. For the bookish memes. The tags on social media. The constant support. The reviews. The emails. The recommendations. The shares on social media. For driving your friends crazy until they read my stories. For buying signed copies. For gifting copies. For the unconditional love for me and all my wild, twisted ideas. For being everything I could've ever hoped for in a fan base. I tell you this a lot, but I've dreamed of each one of you for my entire life. This is my dream. *You* are my dream. Thank you for believing in it, and me, with all you have.

Last but certainly not least, to you—thank you for picking up this book and supporting my art. Whether this is your first Kiersten Modglin book or one of many, thank you for spending a little time with these characters and in this world. Thank you for going on this journey with me. I hope it was everything you wished for and nothing like you expected all at once.

ABOUT THE AUTHOR

Kiersten Modglin is an Amazon Top 30 bestselling author of psychological thrillers, a member of International Thriller Writers and the Alliance of Independent Authors, a KDP Select All-Star, and a ThrillerFix Best Psychological Thriller Award Recipient. Kiersten grew up in rural Western Kentucky with dreams of someday publishing a book or two. With more than twenty-five books published to date, Kiersten now lives in Nashville, Tennessee with her husband, daughter, and their two Boston Terriers: Cedric and Georgie. She is best known for her unpredictable psychological suspense. Kiersten's work is currently being translated into multiple languages and readers across the world refer to her as 'The Queen of Twists.' A Netflix addict, Shonda Rhimes super-fan, psychology fanatic, and indoor enthusiast, Kiersten enjoys rainy days spent with her nose in a book.

Sign up for Kiersten's newsletter here:
http://eepurl.com/b3cNFP
Sign up for text alerts from Kiersten here:
www.kierstenmodglinauthor.com/textalerts.html

www.kierstenmodglinauthor.com
www.facebook.com/kierstenmodglinauthor
www.facebook.com/groups/kmodsquad
www.twitter.com/kmodglinauthor
www.instagram.com/kierstenmodglinauthor
www.tiktok.com/@kierstenmodglinauthor
www.goodreads.com/kierstenmodglinauthor
www.bookbub.com/authors/kiersten-modglin
www.amazon.com/author/kierstenmodglin

ALSO BY KIERSTEN MODGLIN

STANDALONE NOVELS

Becoming Mrs. Abbott

The List

The Missing Piece

Playing Jenna

The Beginning After

The Better Choice

The Good Neighbors

The Lucky Ones

I Said Yes

The Mother-in-Law

The Dream Job

The Liar's Wife

My Husband's Secret

The Perfect Getaway

The Arrangement

The Roommate

The Missing

Just Married

Widow Falls

Missing Daughter

THE MESSES SERIES

The Cleaner (The Messes, #1)

The Healer (The Messes, #2)

The Liar (The Messes, #3)

The Prisoner (The Messes, #4)

NOVELLAS

The Long Route: A Lover's Landing Novella

The Stranger in the Woods: A Crimson Falls Novella

THE LOCKE INDUSTRIES SERIES

The Nanny's Secret

Made in the USA
Monee, IL
04 September 2021

76369129R00142